Selected Stories by
FYODOR DOSTOYEVSKY

Books in this Series:

Selected Stories by
FYODOR DOSTOYEVSKY

RUPA

Published by
Rupa Publications India Pvt. Ltd 2014
7/16, Ansari Road, Daryaganj
New Delhi 110002

Sales Centres:
Allahabad Bengaluru Chennai
Hyderabad Jaipur Kathmandu
Kolkata Mumbai

Selection and Introduction copyright © Terry O'Brien 2014

ISBN: 978-81-291-3521-6

First impression 2014

10 9 8 7 6 5 4 3 2 1

Printed and bound in India by Repro Knowledgecast Limited, Thane

CONTENTS

INTRODUCTION

Fyodor Mikhailovich Dostoyevsky (11 November 1821–9 February 1881) was a Russian novelist, short story writer, essayist and philosopher. Dostoyevsky's literary works explore human psychology in the context of the troubled political, social and spiritual atmosphere of nineteenth century Russia. He has eleven novels, three novellas, seventeen short novels and many other works to his credit. His first novel, *Poor Folk*, was published in 1846 when he was twenty-five. His major works include *Crime and Punishment* (1866), *The Idiot* (1869), and *The Brothers Karamazov* (1880). His books have been translated into more than 170 languages. Dostoyevsky influenced a multitude of writers and philosophers, from Anton Chekhov and Ernest Hemingway to Friedrich Nietzsche and Jean-Paul Sartre.

- 'An Honest Thief' tells the story of how a housekeeper, Agrafena, introduces an old soldier named Astafy Ivanovitch into the household as a lodger, who becomes a companion to the reclusive narrator, breaking the monotony and loneliness of his existence.
- 'The Heavenly Christmas Tree' is a tragic tale of a poor orphan boy, who—lost on a cold Christmas Eve—is shunned by everyone he encounters.
- 'The Peasant Marey' is an autobiographical account in which Dostoyevsky recalls a memory from his early

childhood. The story revolves around a prison camp where a Polish political prisoner—a nobleman—is disgusted at the debauchery of the prisoners around him, and expresses his hatred for the low-bred convicts.

- 'The Crocodile: An Extraordinary Incident' is a fantastical tale about a man swallowed whole by a crocodile, who then decides to carry on his work as a civil servant as best as he can from within the crocodile.

- The story 'Bobok: From Somebody's Diary' is framed as an excerpt from the diary of a frustrated writer named Ivan Ivanovitch. One day he attends the funeral of a casual acquaintance and begins to hear the voices of the recently deceased and buried.

- 'The Dream of a Ridiculous Man' is the story of a man who decides that there is nothing of any value in the world and is therefore determined to commit suicide. A chance encounter with a young girl, however, rejuvenates in him a love for his fellow man.

1

AN HONEST THIEF

One morning, just as I was about to set off to my office, Agrafena, my cook, washerwoman and housekeeper, came in to me and, to my surprise, entered into conversation.

She had always been such a silent, simple creature that, except her daily inquiry about dinner, she had not uttered a word for the last six years. I, at least, had heard nothing else from her.

'Here I have come in to have a word with you, sir,' she began abruptly; 'you really ought to let the little room.'

'Which little room?'

'Why, the one next the kitchen, to be sure.'

'What for?'

'What for? Why because folks do take in lodgers, to be sure.'

'But who would take it?'

'Who would take it? Why, a lodger would take it, to be sure.'

'But, my good woman, one could not put a bedstead in it; there wouldn't be room to move! Who could live in it?'

'Who wants to live there! As long as he has a place to sleep in. Why, he would live in the window.'

'In what window?'

'In what window! As though you didn't know! The one in the passage, to be sure. He would sit there, sewing or doing anything else. Maybe he would sit on a chair, too. He's got a chair; and he has a table, too; he's got everything.'

'Who is "he" then?'

'Oh, a good man, a man of experience. I will cook for him. And I'll ask him three roubles a month for his board and lodging.'

After prolonged efforts I succeeded at last in learning from Agrafena that an elderly man had somehow managed to persuade her to admit him into the kitchen as a lodger and boarder. Any notion Agrafena took into her head had to be carried out; if not, I knew she would give me no peace. When anything was not to her liking, she at once began to brood, and sank into a deep dejection that would last for a fortnight or three weeks. During that period my dinners were spoiled, my linen was mislaid, my floors went unscrubbed; in short, I had a great deal to put up with. I had observed long ago that this inarticulate woman was incapable of conceiving a project, of originating an idea of her own. But if anything like a notion or a project was by some means put into her feeble brain, to prevent its being carried out meant, for a time, her moral assassination. And so, as I cared more for my peace of mind than for anything else, I consented forthwith.

'Has he a passport anyway, or something of the sort?'

'To be sure, he has. He is a good man, a man of experience; three roubles he's promised to pay.'

The very next day the new lodger made his appearance in my modest bachelor quarters; but I was not put out by this, indeed I was inwardly pleased. I lead as a rule a very lonely hermit's existence. I have scarcely any friends; I hardly ever go anywhere. As I had spent ten years never coming out of my shell, I had, of course, grown used to solitude. But another ten or fifteen years or more of the same solitary existence, with the same Agrafena, in the same bachelor quarters, was in truth a somewhat cheerless prospect. And therefore a new inmate, if well-behaved, was a heaven-sent blessing.

Agrafena had spoken truly: my lodger was certainly a man of experience. From his passport it appeared that he was an old soldier, a fact which I should have known indeed from his face. An old soldier is easily recognized. Astafy Ivanovitch was a favourable specimen of his class. We got on very well together. What was best of all, Astafy Ivanovitch would sometimes tell a story, describing some incident in his own life. In the perpetual boredom of my existence such a storyteller was a veritable treasure. One day he told me one of these stories. It made an impression on me. The following event was what led to it.

I was left alone in the flat; both Astafy and Agrafena were out on business of their own. All of a sudden I heard from the inner room somebody—I fancied a stranger—come in; I went out; there actually was a stranger in the passage, a short fellow wearing no overcoat in spite of the cold autumn weather.

'What do you want?'

'Does a clerk called Alexandrov live here?'

'Nobody of that name here, brother. Good-bye.'

'Why, the dvornik told me it was here,' said my visitor, cautiously retiring towards the door.

'Be off, be off, brother, get along.'

Next day after dinner, while Astafy Ivanovitch was fitting on a coat which he was altering for me, again some one came into the passage. I half opened the door.

Before my very eyes my yesterday's visitor, with perfect composure, took my wadded greatcoat from the peg and, stuffing it under his arm, darted out of the flat. Agrafena stood all the time staring at him, agape with astonishment and doing nothing for the protection of my property. Astafy Ivanovitch flew in pursuit of the thief and ten minutes later came back out of breath and empty-handed. He had vanished completely.

'Well, there's a piece of luck, Astafy Ivanovitch!'

'It's a good job your cloak is left! Or he would have put you in a plight, the thief!'

But the whole incident had so impressed Astafy Ivanovitch that I forgot the theft as I looked at him. He could not get over it. Every minute or two he would drop the work upon which he was engaged, and would describe over again how it had all happened, how he had been standing, how the greatcoat had been taken down before his very eyes, not a yard away, and how it had come to pass that he could not catch the thief. Then he would sit down to his work again, then leave it once more, and at last I saw him go down to the dvornik to tell him all about it, and to upbraid him for letting such a thing happen in his domain. Then he came back and began scolding Agrafena. Then he sat down to his work again, and long afterwards he was still muttering to himself how it had all happened, how he stood there and I was here, how before our eyes, not a yard away, the thief took the coat off the peg, and so on. In short, though Astafy Ivanovitch understood his business, he was a terrible slowcoach and busybody.

'He's made fools of us, Astafy Ivanovitch,' I said to him in the evening, as I gave him a glass of tea. I wanted to while away the time by recalling the story of the lost greatcoat, the frequent repetition of which, together with the great earnestness of the speaker, was beginning to become very amusing.

'Fools, indeed, sir! Even though it is no business of mine, I am put out. It makes me angry though it is not my coat that was lost. To my thinking there is no vermin in the world worse than a thief. Another takes what you can spare, but a thief steals the work of your hands, the sweat of your brow, your time... Ugh, it's nasty! One can't speak of it! It's too vexing. How is it you don't feel the loss of your property, sir?'

'Yes, you are right, Astafy Ivanovitch, better if the thing had been burnt; it's annoying to let the thief have it, it's disagreeable.'

'Disagreeable! I should think so! Yet, to be sure, there are thieves and thieves. And I have happened, sir, to come across an honest thief.'

'An honest thief? But how can a thief be honest, Astafy Ivanovitch?'

'There you are right indeed, sir. How can a thief be honest? There are none such. I only meant to say that he was an honest man, sure enough, and yet he stole. I was simply sorry for him.'

'Why, how was that, Astafy Ivanovitch?'

'It was about two years ago, sir. I had been nearly a year out of a place, and just before I lost my place I made the acquaintance of a poor lost creature. We got acquainted in a public house. He was a drunkard, a vagrant, a beggar, he had been in a situation of some sort, but from his drinking habits he had lost his work. Such a ne'er-do-well! God only knows what he had on! Often you wouldn't be sure if he'd a shirt under his coat; everything he could lay his hands upon he would drink away. But he was not one to quarrel; he was a quiet fellow. A soft, good-natured chap. And he'd never ask, he was ashamed; but you could see for yourself the poor fellow wanted a drink, and you would stand it him. And so we got friendly, that's to say, he stuck to me... It was all one to me. And what a man he was, to be sure! Like a little dog he would follow me; wherever I went there he would be; and all that after our first meeting, and he as thin as a thread-paper! At first it was "let me stay the night"; well, I let him stay.

'I looked at his passport, too; the man was all right.

'Well, the next day it was the same story, and then the third day he came again and sat all day in the window and stayed the night. Well, thinks I, he is sticking to me; give him food and drink and shelter at night, too—here am I, a poor man, and a hanger-on to keep as well! And before he came to me, he used to go in the same way to a government clerk's; he attached himself to him; they were always drinking together; but he, through trouble of some sort, drank himself into the grave. My man was called Emelyan Ilyitch. I pondered and pondered what I was to do with him. To drive him away I was ashamed. I was sorry for him; such a pitiful, godforsaken creature I never did set eyes on. And not a word said either; he does not ask, but just sits there and looks into your eyes like a dog. To think what drinking will bring a man down to!

'I keep asking myself how am I to say to him: "You must be moving, Emelyanoushka, there's nothing for you here, you've come to the wrong place; I shall soon not have a bite for myself, how am I to keep you too?"

'I sat and wondered what he'd do when I said that to him. And I seemed to see how he'd stare at me, if he were to hear me say that, how long he would sit and not understand a word of it. And when it did get home to him at last, how he would get up from the window, would take up his bundle—I can see it now, the red-check handkerchief full of holes, with God knows what wrapped up in it, which he had always with him, and then how he would set his shabby old coat to rights, so that it would look decent and keep him warm, so that no holes would be seen—he was a man of delicate feelings! And how he'd open the door and go out with tears in his eyes. Well, there's no letting a man go to ruin like that... One's sorry for him.

'And then again, I think, how am I off myself? Wait a bit, Emelyanoushka, says I to myself, you've not long to feast with me: I shall soon be going away and then you will not find me.

'Well, sir, our family made a move; and Alexandr Filimonovitch, my master (now deceased, God rest his soul), said, "I am thoroughly satisfied with you, Astafy Ivanovitch; when we come back from the country we will take you on again." I had been butler with them; a nice gentleman he was, but he died that same year. Well, after seeing him off, I took my belongings, what little money I had, and I thought I'd have a rest for a time, so I went to an old woman I knew, and I took a corner in her room. There was only one corner free in it. She had been a nurse, so now she had a pension and a room of her own. Well, now good-bye, Emelyanoushka, thinks I, you won't find me now, my boy.

'And what do you think, sir? I had gone out to see a man I knew, and when I came back in the evening, the first thing I saw was Emelyanoushka! There he was, sitting on my box and his check bundle beside him; he was sitting in his ragged old coat, waiting for me. And to while away the time he had borrowed a church book from the old lady, and was holding it wrong side upwards. He'd scented me out! My heart sank. Well, thinks I, there's no help for it—why didn't I turn him out at first? So I asked him straight off: "Have you brought your passport, Emelyanoushka?"

'I sat down on the spot, sir, and began to ponder: will a vagabond like that be very much trouble to me? And on thinking it over it seemed he would not be much trouble. He must be fed, I thought. Well, a bit of bread in the morning, and to make it go down better I'll buy him an onion. At midday I should have to give him another bit of bread and an onion; and in the evening, onion again with kvass, with some more bread if he wanted it. And if some cabbage soup were to come our way, then we should both have had our fill. I am no great eater myself, and a drinking man, as we all know, never eats; all he wants is herb-brandy or green vodka. He'll ruin me with his drinking, I thought, but then another idea came into my head, sir, and took great hold on me. So much so that if

Emelyanoushka had gone away I should have felt that I had nothing to live for, I do believe... I determined on the spot to be a father and guardian to him. I'll keep him from ruin, I thought, I'll wean him from the glass! You wait a bit, thought I; very well, Emelyanoushka, you may stay, only you must behave yourself; you must obey orders.

'Well, thinks I to myself, I'll begin by training him to work of some sort, but not all at once; let him enjoy himself a little first, and I'll look round and find something you are fit for, Emelyanoushka. For every sort of work a man needs a special ability, you know, sir. And I began to watch him on the quiet; I soon saw Emelyanoushka was a desperate character. I began, sir, with a word of advice: I said this and that to him. "Emelyanoushka," said I, "you ought to take a thought and mend your ways. Have done with drinking! Just look what rags you go about in: that old coat of yours, if I may make bold to say so, is fit for nothing but a sieve. A pretty state of things! It's time to draw the line, sure enough." Emelyanoushka sat and listened to me with his head hanging down. Would you believe it, sir? It had come to such a pass with him, he'd lost his tongue through drink and could not speak a word of sense. Talk to him of cucumbers and he'd answer back about beans! He would listen and listen to me and then heave such a sigh. "What are you sighing for, Emelyan Ilyitch?" I asked him.

'"Oh, nothing; don't you mind me, Astafy Ivanovitch. Do you know there were two women fighting in the street today, Astafy Ivanovitch? One upset the other woman's basket of cranberries by accident."

'"Well, what of that?"

'"And the second one upset the other's cranberries on purpose and trampled them under foot, too."

'"Well, and what of it, Emelyan Ilyitch?"

'"Why, nothing, Astafy Ivanovitch, I just mentioned it."

"'Nothing, I just mentioned it!' Emelyanoushka, my boy, I thought, you've squandered and drunk away your brains!"

'And do you know, a gentleman dropped a money-note on the pavement in Gorohovy Street, no, it was Sadovy Street. And a peasant saw it and said, 'That's my luck'; and at the same time another man saw it and said, 'No, it's my bit of luck. I saw it before you did.'"

"'Well, Emelyan Ilyitch?'"

"'And the fellows had a fight over it, Astafy Ivanovitch. But a policeman came up, took away the note, gave it back to the gentleman and threatened to take up both the men.'"

"'Well, but what of that? What is there edifying about it, Emelyanoushka?'"

"'Why, nothing, to be sure. Folks laughed, Astafy Ivanovitch.'"

"'Ach, Emelyanoushka! What do the folks matter? You've sold your soul for a brass farthing! But do you know what I have to tell you, Emelyan Ilyitch?'"

"'What, Astafy Ivanovitch?'"

"'Take a job of some sort, that's what you must do. For the hundredth time I say to you, set to work, have some mercy on yourself!'"

"'What could I set to, Astafy Ivanovitch? I don't know what job I could set to, and there is no one who will take me on, Astafy Ivanovitch.'"

"'That's how you came to be turned off, Emelyanoushka, you drinking man!'"

"'And do you know Vlass, the waiter, was sent for to the office today, Astafy Ivanovitch?'"

"'Why did they send for him, Emelyanoushka?' I asked."

"'I could not say why, Astafy Ivanovitch. I suppose they wanted him there, and that's why they sent for him.'"

'A-ach, thought I, we are in a bad way, poor Emelyanoushka! The Lord is chastising us for our sins. Well, sir, what is one to do with such a man?

'But a cunning fellow he was, and no mistake. He'd listen and listen to me, but at last I suppose he got sick of it. As soon as he sees I am beginning to get angry, he'd pick up his old coat and out he'd slip and leave no trace. He'd wander about all day and come back at night drunk. Where he got the money from, the Lord only knows; I had no hand in that.

'"No," said I, "Emelyan Ilyitch, you'll come to a bad end. Give over drinking, mind what I say now, give it up! Next time you come home in liquor, you can spend the night on the stairs. I won't let you in!"

'After hearing that threat, Emelyanoushka sat at home that day and the next; but on the third he slipped off again. I waited and waited; he didn't come back. Well, at least I don't mind owning, I was in a fright, and I felt for the man too. What have I done to him? I thought. I've scared him away. Where's the poor fellow gone to now? He'll get lost maybe. Lord have mercy upon us!

'Night came on, he did not come. In the morning I went out into the porch; I looked, and if he hadn't gone to sleep in the porch! There he was with his head on the step, and chilled to the marrow of his bones.

'"What next, Emelyanoushka, God have mercy on you! Where will you get to next!"

'"Why, you were—sort of—angry with me, Astafy Ivanovitch, the other day, you were vexed and promised to put me to sleep in the porch, so I didn't—sort of—venture to come in, Astafy Ivanovitch, and so I lay down here…"

'I did feel angry and sorry too.

'"Surely you might undertake some other duty, Emelyanoushka, instead of lying here guarding the steps," I said.

'"Why, what other duty, Astafy Ivanovitch?"

'"You lost soul"—I was in such a rage, I called him that—"if you could but learn tailoring work! Look at your old rag of a coat! It's not enough to have it in tatters, here you are sweeping the steps with it! You might take a needle and boggle up your rags, as decency demands. Ah, you drunken man!"

'What do you think, sir? He actually did take a needle. Of course I said it in jest, but he was so scared he set to work. He took off his coat and began threading the needle. I watched him; as you may well guess, his eyes were all red and bleary, and his hands were all of a shake. He kept shoving and shoving the thread and could not get it through the eye of the needle; he kept screwing his eyes up and wetting the thread and twisting it in his fingers—it was no good! He gave it up and looked at me.

'"Well," said I, "this is a nice way to treat me! If there had been folks by to see, I don't know what I should have done! Why, you simple fellow, I said it you in joke, as a reproach. Give over your nonsense, God bless you! Sit quiet and don't put me to shame, don't sleep on my stairs and make a laughing-stock of me."

'"Why, what am I to do, Astafy Ivanovitch? I know very well I am a drunkard and good for nothing! I can do nothing but vex you, my bene—bene—factor…"

'And at that his blue lips began all of a sudden to quiver, and a tear ran down his white cheek and trembled on his stubbly chin, and then poor Emelyanoushka burst into a regular flood of tears. Mercy on us! I felt as though a knife were thrust into my heart! The sensitive creature! I'd never have expected it. Who could have guessed it? No, Emelyanoushka, thought I, I shall give you up altogether. You can go your way like the rubbish you are.

'Well, sir, why make a long story of it? And the whole affair is so trifling; it's not worth wasting words upon. Why, you, for instance, sir, would not have given a thought to it, but I would have given a great deal—if I had a great deal to give—that it never should have happened at all.

'I had a pair of riding breeches by me, sir, deuce take them, fine, first-rate riding breeches they were too, blue with a check on it. They'd been ordered by a gentleman from the country, but he would not have them after all; said they were not full enough, so they were left on my hands. It struck me they were worth something. At the second-hand dealer's I ought to get five silver roubles for them, or if not I could turn them into two pairs of trousers for Petersburg gentlemen and have a piece over for a waistcoat for myself. Of course for poor people like us everything comes in. And it happened just then that Emelyanoushka was having a sad time of it. There he sat day after day: he did not drink, not a drop passed his lips, but he sat and moped like an owl. It was sad to see him—he just sat and brooded. Well, thought I, either you've not got a copper to spend, my lad, or else you're turning over a new leaf of yourself, you've given it up, you've listened to reason. Well, sir, that's how it was with us; and just then came a holiday. I went to vespers; when I came home I found Emelyanoushka sitting in the window, drunk and rocking to and fro.

'Ah! So that's what you've been up to, my lad! And I went to get something out of my chest. And when I looked in, the breeches were not there... I rummaged here and there; they'd vanished. When I'd ransacked everywhere and saw they were not there, something seemed to stab me to the heart. I ran first to the old dame and began accusing her; of Emelyanoushka I'd not the faintest suspicion, though there was cause for it in his sitting there drunk.

'"No," said the old body, "God be with you, my fine gentleman, what good are riding breeches to me? Am I going to wear such things? Why, a skirt I had I lost the other day through a fellow of your sort...I know nothing; I can tell you nothing about it," she said.

"'Who has been here, who has been in?" I asked.

"'Why, nobody has been, my good sir," says she; "I've been here all the while; Emelyan Ilyitch went out and came back again; there he sits, ask him."

"Emelyanoushka," said I, "have you taken those new riding breeches for anything; you remember the pair I made for that gentleman from the country?"

"'No, Astafy Ivanovitch," said he; "I've not—sort of—touched them."

'I was in a state! I hunted high and low for them—they were nowhere to be found. And Emelyanoushka sits there rocking himself to and fro. I was squatting on my heels facing him and bending over the chest, and all at once I stole a glance at him... Alack, I thought; my heart suddenly grew hot within me and I felt myself flushing up too. And suddenly Emelyanoushka looked at me.

"'No, Astafy Ivanovitch," said he, "those riding breeches of yours, maybe, you are thinking, maybe, I took them, but I never touched them."

"'But what can have become of them, Emelyan Ilyitch?"

"'No, Astafy Ivanovitch," said he, "I've never seen them."

"'Why, Emelyan Ilyitch, I suppose they've run off of themselves, eh?"

"'Maybe they have, Astafy Ivanovitch."

'When I heard him say that, I got up at once, went up to him, lighted the lamp and sat down to work to my sewing. I was altering a waistcoat for a clerk who lived below us. And wasn't there a burning pain and ache in my breast! I shouldn't have minded so much if I had put all the clothes I had in the fire. Emelyanoushka seemed to have an inkling of what a rage I was in. When a man is guilty, you know, sir, he scents trouble far off, like the birds of the air before a storm.

'"Do you know what, Astafy Ivanovitch," Emelyanoushka began, and his poor old voice was shaking as he said the words, "Antip Prohoritch, the apothecary, married the coachman's wife this morning, who died the other day—"

'I did give him a look, sir, a nasty look it was; Emelyanoushka understood it too. I saw him get up, go to the bed, and begin to rummage there for something. I waited—he was busy there a long time and kept muttering all the while, "No, not there, where can the blessed things have got to!" I waited to see what he'd do; I saw him creep under the bed on all fours. I couldn't bear it any longer. "What are you crawling about under the bed for, Emelyan Ilyitch?" said I.

'"Looking for the breeches, Astafy Ivanovitch. Maybe they've dropped down there somewhere."

'"Why should you try to help a poor simple man like me," said I, "crawling on your knees for nothing, sir?"—I called him that in my vexation.

'"Oh, never mind, Astafy Ivanovitch, I'll just look. They'll turn up, maybe, somewhere."

'"H'm," said I, "look here, Emelyan Ilyitch!"

'"What is it, Astafy Ivanovitch?" said he.

'"Haven't you simply stolen them from me like a thief and a robber, in return for the bread and salt you've eaten here?" said I.

'I felt so angry, sir, at seeing him fooling about on his knees before me.

'"No, Astafy Ivanovitch."

'And he stayed lying as he was on his face under the bed. A long time he lay there and then at last crept out. I looked at him and the man was as white as a sheet. He stood up, and sat down near me in the window and sat so for some ten minutes.

'"No, Astafy Ivanovitch," he said, and all at once he stood up and came towards me, and I can see him now; he looked dreadful. "No, Astafy Ivanovitch," said he, "I never—sort of—touched your breeches."

'He was all of a shake, poking himself in the chest with a trembling finger, and his poor old voice shook so that I was frightened, sir, and sat as though I was rooted to the window-seat.

'"Well, Emelyan Ilyitch," said I, "as you will, forgive me if I, in my foolishness, have accused you unjustly. As for the breeches, let them go hang; we can live without them. We've still our hands, thank God; we need not go thieving or begging from some other poor man; we'll earn our bread."

'Emelyanoushka heard me out and went on standing there before me. I looked up, and he had sat down. And there he sat all the evening without stirring. At last I lay down to sleep. Emelyanoushka went on sitting in the same place. When I looked out in the morning, he was lying curled up in his old coat on the bare floor; he felt too crushed even to come to bed. Well, sir, I felt no more liking for the fellow from that day, in fact for the first few days I hated him. I felt as one may say as though my own son had robbed me, and done me a deadly hurt. Ach, thought I, Emelyanoushka, Emelyanoushka! And Emelyanoushka, sir, went on drinking for a whole fortnight without stopping. He was drunk all the time, and regularly besotted. He went out in the morning and came back late at night, and for a whole fortnight I didn't get a word out of him. It was as though grief was gnawing at his heart, or as though he wanted to do for himself completely. At last he stopped; he must have come to the end of all he'd got, and then he sat in the window again. I remember he sat there without speaking for three days and three nights; all of a sudden I saw that he was crying. He was just sitting there, sir, and crying like anything; a perfect stream, as though he didn't know how his tears were flowing. And it's a sad thing, sir, to see a grown-up man and an old man, too, crying from woe and grief.

"'What's the matter, Emelyanoushka?" said I.

'He began to tremble so that he shook all over. I spoke to him for the first time since that evening.

"'Nothing, Astafy Ivanovitch."

"'God be with you, Emelyanoushka, what's lost is lost. Why are you moping about like this?" I felt sorry for him.

"'Oh, nothing, Astafy Ivanovitch, it's no matter. I want to find some work to do, Astafy Ivanovitch."

"'And what sort of work, pray, Emelyanoushka?"

"'Why, any sort; perhaps I could find a situation such as I used to have. I've been already to ask Fedosay Ivanitch. I don't like to be a burden on you, Astafy Ivanovitch. If I can find a situation, Astafy Ivanovitch, then I'll pay it you all back, and make you a return for all your hospitality."

"'Enough, Emelyanoushka, enough; let bygones be bygones—and no more to be said about it. Let us go on as we used to do before."

"'No, Astafy Ivanovitch, you, maybe, think—but I never touched your riding breeches."

"'Well, have it your own way; God be with you, Emelyanoushka."

"'No, Astafy Ivanovitch, I can't go on living with you, that's clear. You must excuse me, Astafy Ivanovitch."

"'Why, God bless you, Emelyan Ilyitch, who's offending you and driving you out of the place—am I doing it?"

"'No, it's not the proper thing for me to live with you like this, Astafy Ivanovitch. I'd better be going."

'He was so hurt, it seemed, he stuck to his point. I looked at him, and sure enough, up he got and pulled his old coat over his shoulders.

"'But where are you going, Emelyan Ilyitch? Listen to reason: what are you about? Where are you off to?"

'"No, good-bye, Astafy Ivanovitch, don't keep me now"—and he was blubbering again—"I'd better be going. You're not the same now."

'"Not the same as what? I am the same. But you'll be lost by yourself like a poor helpless babe, Emelyan Ilyitch."

'"No, Astafy Ivanovitch, when you go out now, you lock up your chest and it makes me cry to see it, Astafy Ivanovitch. You'd better let me go, Astafy Ivanovitch, and forgive me all the trouble I've given you while I've been living with you."

'Well, sir, the man went away. I waited for a day; I expected he'd be back in the evening—no. Next day no sign of him, nor the third day either. I began to get frightened; I was so worried, I couldn't drink, I couldn't eat, I couldn't sleep. The fellow had quite disarmed me. On the fourth day I went out to look for him; I peeped into all the taverns, to inquire for him—but no, Emelyanoushka was lost. "Have you managed to keep yourself alive, Emelyanoushka?" I wondered. "Perhaps he is lying dead under some hedge, poor drunkard, like a sodden log." I went home more dead than alive. Next day I went out to look for him again. And I kept cursing myself that I'd been such a fool as to let the man go off by himself. On the fifth day it was a holiday—in the early morning I heard the door creak. I looked up and there was my Emelyanoushka coming in. His face was blue and his hair was covered with dirt as though he'd been sleeping in the street; he was as thin as a match. He took off his old coat, sat down on the chest and looked at me. I was delighted to see him, but I felt more upset about him than ever. For you see, sir, if I'd been overtaken in some sin, as true as I am here, sir, I'd have died like a dog before I'd have come back. But Emelyanoushka did come back. And a sad thing it was, sure enough, to see a man sunk so low. I began to look after him, to talk kindly to him, to comfort him.

'"Well, Emelyanoushka," said I, "I am glad you've come

back. Had you been away much longer I should have gone to look for you in the taverns again today. Are you hungry?'

"'No, Astafy Ivanovitch."

"'Come, now, aren't you really? Here, brother, is some cabbage soup left over from yesterday; there was meat in it; it is good stuff. And here is some bread and onion. Come, eat it, it'll do you no harm."

'I made him eat it, and I saw at once that the man had not tasted food for maybe three days—he was as hungry as a wolf. So it was hunger that had driven him to me. My heart was melted looking at the poor dear. "Let me run to the tavern," thought I, "I'll get something to ease his heart, and then we'll make an end of it. I've no more anger in my heart against you, Emelyanoushka!" I brought him some vodka. "Here, Emelyan Ilyitch, let us have a drink for the holiday. Like a drink? And it will do you good." He held out his hand, held it out greedily; he was just taking it, and then he stopped himself. But a minute after I saw him take it, and lift it to his mouth, spilling it on his sleeve. But though he got it to his lips he set it down on the table again.

"'What is it, Emelyanoushka?"

"'Nothing, Astafy Ivanovitch, I—sort of—"

"'Won't you drink it?"

"'Well, Astafy Ivanovitch, I'm not—sort of—going to drink any more, Astafy Ivanovitch."

"'Do you mean you've given it up altogether, Emelyanoushka, or are you only not going to drink today?"

'He did not answer. A minute later I saw him rest his head on his hand.

"'What's the matter, Emelyanoushka, are you ill?"

"'Why, yes, Astafy Ivanovitch, I don't feel well."

'I took him and laid him down on the bed. I saw that he really was ill: his head was burning hot and he was shivering with fever. I sat by him all day; towards night he was worse. I mixed him some oil and onion and kvass and bread broken up.

'"Come, eat some of this," said I, "and perhaps you'll be better." He shook his head. "No," said he, "I won't have any dinner today, Astafy Ivanovitch."

'I made some tea for him, I quite flustered our old woman—he was no better. Well, thinks I, it's a bad look-out! The third morning I went for a medical gentleman. There was one I knew living close by, Kostopravov by name. I'd made his acquaintance when I was in service with the Bosomyagins; he'd attended me. The doctor came and looked at him. "He's in a bad way," said he, "it was no use sending for me. But if you like I can give him a powder." Well, I didn't give him a powder, I thought that's just the doctor's little game; and then the fifth day came.

'He lay, sir, dying before my eyes. I sat in the window with my work in my hands. The old woman was heating the stove. We were all silent. My heart was simply breaking over him, the good-for-nothing fellow; I felt as if it were a son of my own I was losing. I knew that Emelyanoushka was looking at me. I'd seen the man all the day long making up his mind to say something and not daring to.

'At last I looked up at him; I saw such misery in the poor fellow's eyes. He had kept them fixed on me, but when he saw that I was looking at him, he looked down at once.

'"Astafy Ivanovitch."

'"What is it, Emelyanoushka?"

'"If you were to take my old coat to a second-hand dealer's, how much do you think they'd give you for it, Astafy Ivanovitch?"

'"There's no knowing how much they'd give. Maybe they would give me a rouble for it, Emelyan Ilyitch."

'But if I had taken it they wouldn't have given a farthing for it, but would have laughed in my face for bringing such a trumpery thing. I simply said that to comfort the poor fellow, knowing the simpleton he was.

"'But I was thinking, Astafy Ivanovitch, they might give you three roubles for it; it's made of cloth, Astafy Ivanovitch. How could they only give one rouble for a cloth coat?'

"'I don't know, Emelyan Ilyitch,' said I, 'if you are thinking of taking it you should certainly ask three roubles to begin with.'

'Emelyanoushka was silent for a time, and then he addressed me again—

"'Astafy Ivanovitch.'

"'What is it, Emelyanoushka?' I asked.

"'Sell my coat when I die, and don't bury me in it. I can lie as well without it; and it's a thing of some value—it might come in useful.'

'I can't tell you how it made my heart ache to hear him. I saw that the death agony was coming on him. We were silent again for a bit. So an hour passed by. I looked at him again: he was still staring at me, and when he met my eyes he looked down again.

"'Do you want some water to drink, Emelyan Ilyitch?' I asked.

"'Give me some, God bless you, Astafy Ivanovitch.'

'I gave him a drink.

"'Thank you, Astafy Ivanovitch,' said he.

"'Is there anything else you would like, Emelyanoushka?'

"'No, Astafy Ivanovitch, there's nothing I want, but I—sort of—'

"'What?'

"'I only—'

"'What is it, Emelyanoushka?'

"'Those riding breeches—it was—sort of—I who took them—Astafy Ivanovitch.'

'"Well, God forgive you, Emelyanoushka," said I, "you poor, sorrowful creature. Depart in peace."

'And I was choking myself, sir, and the tears were in my eyes. I turned aside for a moment.

"Astafy Ivanovitch—"

'I saw Emelyanoushka wanted to tell me something; he was trying to sit up, trying to speak, and mumbling something. He flushed red all over suddenly, looked at me...then I saw him turn white again, whiter and whiter, and he seemed to sink away all in a minute. His head fell back, he drew one breath and gave up his soul to God.'

2

THE HEAVENLY CHRISTMAS TREE

I am a novelist, and I suppose I have made up this story. I write 'I suppose,' though I know for a fact that I have made it up, but yet I keep fancying that it must have happened somewhere at some time, that it must have happened on Christmas Eve in some great town in a time of terrible frost.

I have a vision of a boy, a little boy, six years old or even younger. This boy woke up that morning in a cold damp cellar. He was dressed in a sort of little dressing-gown and was shivering with cold. There was a cloud of white steam from his breath, and sitting on a box in the corner, he blew the steam out of his mouth and amused himself in his dullness watching it float away. But he was terribly hungry. Several times that morning he went up to the plank bed where his sick mother was lying on a mattress as thin as a pancake, with some sort of bundle under her head for a pillow. How had she come here? She must have come with her boy from some other town and suddenly fallen ill. The landlady who let the 'corners' had been taken two days before to the police station, the lodgers were out and about as the holiday was so near, and the only one left had been lying for the last twenty-four hours dead drunk, not having waited for Christmas. In another corner of the room a wretched old woman of eighty, who had once been a children's nurse but was now left to die friendless, was moaning and groaning with rheumatism, scolding and grumbling at the boy so that he was afraid to go near her corner. He had got a drink of water in the outer room, but could not find a crust anywhere, and had been on the point of waking his mother a dozen times. He felt frightened at last in the darkness: it had long been dusk, but no light was kindled. Touching his mother's face, he was surprised that she did not move at all, and that she was as cold as the wall. 'It is very cold here,' he thought. He stood a little, unconsciously letting his hands rest on the dead woman's shoulders, then he breathed on his fingers to warm them, and then quietly fumbling for his cap on the bed, he went out of the cellar. He would have gone earlier, but was afraid of the big dog which had been howling all day at the neighbour's door at the top of the stairs. But the dog was not there now, and he went out into the street.

Mercy on us, what a town! He had never seen anything like it before. In the town from which he had come, it was always such black darkness at night. There was one lamp for the whole street, the little, low-pitched, wooden houses were closed up with shutters, there was no one to be seen in the street after dusk, all the people shut themselves up in their houses, and there was nothing but the howling of packs of dogs, hundreds and thousands of them barking and howling all night. But there it was so warm and he was given food, while here—oh, dear, if he only had something to eat! And what a noise and rattle here, what light and what people, horses and carriages, and what a frost! The frozen steam hung in clouds over the horses, over their warmly breathing mouths; their hoofs clanged against the stones through the powdery snow, and every one pushed so, and—oh, dear, how he longed for some morsel to eat, and how wretched he suddenly felt. A policeman walked by and turned away to avoid seeing the boy.

Here was another street—oh, what a wide one, here he would be run over for certain; how everyone was shouting, racing and driving along, and the light, the light! And what was this? A huge glass window, and through the window a tree reaching up to the ceiling; it was a fir tree, and on it were ever so many lights, gold papers and apples and little dolls and horses; and there were children clean and dressed in their best running about the room, laughing and playing and eating and drinking something. And then a little girl began dancing with one of the boys, what a pretty little girl! And he could hear the music through the window. The boy looked and wondered and laughed, though his toes were aching with the cold and his fingers were red and stiff so that it hurt him to move them. And all at once the boy remembered how his toes and fingers hurt him, and began crying, and ran on; and again through another windowpane he saw another Christmas tree, and on a table cakes of all sorts—almond cakes, red cakes and yellow cakes, and three grand young ladies were sitting there, and they gave the cakes to any one who went up to them, and the door kept opening, lots of gentlemen and ladies went in from the street. The boy crept up, suddenly opened the door and went in. Oh, how they shouted at him and waved him back! One lady went up to him hurriedly and slipped a kopeck into his hand, and with her own hands opened the door into the street for him! How frightened he was. And the kopeck rolled away and clinked upon the steps; he could not bend his red fingers to hold it tight. The boy ran away and went on, where he did not know. He was ready to cry again but he was afraid, and ran on and on and blew his fingers. And he was miserable because he felt suddenly so lonely and terrified, and all at once, mercy on us! What was this again? People were standing in a crowd admiring. Behind a glass window there were three little dolls, dressed in red and green dresses, and exactly, exactly as though they were alive. One was a little old man sitting and playing a big violin, the two others were standing close by and playing little violins and nodding in time, and looking at one another, and their lips moved, they were speaking, actually speaking, only one couldn't hear through the glass. And at first the boy thought they were alive, and when he grasped that they were dolls he laughed. He had never seen such dolls before, and had no idea there were such dolls! And he wanted to cry, but he felt amused, amused by the dolls. All at once he fancied that some one caught at his smock behind: a wicked big boy was standing beside him and suddenly hit him on the head, snatched off his cap and tripped him up. The boy fell down on the ground, at once there was a shout, he was numb with fright, he jumped up and ran away. He ran, and not knowing where he was going, ran in at the gate of some one's courtyard, and sat down behind a stack of wood: 'They won't find me here, besides it's dark!'

He sat huddled up and was breathless from fright, and all at once, quite suddenly, he felt so happy: his hands and feet suddenly left off aching and grew so warm, as warm as though he were on a stove; then he shivered all over, then he gave a start, why, he must have been asleep. How nice to have a sleep here! 'I'll sit here a little and go and look at the dolls again,' said the boy, and smiled thinking of them. 'Just as though they were alive!...' And suddenly he heard his mother singing over him. 'Mammy, I am asleep; how nice it is to sleep here!'

'Come to my Christmas tree, little one,' a soft voice suddenly whispered over his head.

He thought that this was still his mother, but no, it was not she. Who it was calling him, he could not see, but some one bent over and embraced him in the darkness; and he stretched out his hands to him, and...and all at once—oh, what a bright light! Oh, what a Christmas tree! And yet it was not a fir tree, he had never seen a tree like that! Where was he now? Everything was bright and shining, and all round him were dolls; but no, they were not dolls, they were little boys and girls, only so bright and shining. They all came flying round him, they all kissed him, took him and carried him along with them, and he was flying himself, and he saw that his mother was looking at him and laughing joyfully. 'Mammy, Mammy; oh, how nice it is here, Mammy!' And again he kissed the children and wanted to tell them at once of those dolls in the shop window. 'Who are you, boys? Who are you, girls?' he asked, laughing and admiring them.

'This is Christ's Christmas tree,' they answered. 'Christ always has a Christmas tree on this day, for the little children who have no tree of their own...' And he found out that all these little boys and girls were children just like himself; that some had been frozen in the baskets in which they had as babies been laid on the doorsteps of well-to-do Petersburg people, others had been boarded out with Finnish women by the Foundling and had been suffocated, others had died at their starved mother's breasts (in the Samara famine), others had died in the third-class railway carriages from the foul air; and yet they were all here, they were all like angels about Christ, and He was in the midst of them and held out His hands to them and blessed them and their sinful mothers... And the mothers of these children stood on one side weeping; each one knew her boy or girl, and the children flew up to them and kissed them and wiped away their tears with their little hands, and begged them not to weep because they were so happy.

And down below in the morning the porter found the little dead body of the frozen child on the woodstack; they sought out his mother too... She had died before him. They met before the Lord God in heaven.

Why have I made up such a story, so out of keeping with an ordinary diary, and a writer's above all? And I promised two stories dealing with real events! But that is just it, I keep fancying that all this may have happened really—that is, what took place in the cellar and on the woodstack; but as for Christ's Christmas tree, I cannot tell you whether that could have happened or not.

3

THE PEASANT MAREY

It was the second day in Easter week. The air was warm, the sky was blue, the sun was high, warm, bright, but my soul was very gloomy. I sauntered behind the prison barracks. I stared at the palings of the stout prison fence, counting the movers; but I had no inclination to count them, though it was my habit to do so. This was the second day of the 'holidays' in the prison; the convicts were not taken out to work, there were numbers of men drunk, loud abuse and quarrelling was springing up continually in every corner. There were hideous, disgusting songs and card-parties installed beside the platform-beds. Several of the convicts who had been sentenced by their comrades, for special violence, to be beaten till they were half dead, were lying on the platform-bed, covered with sheepskins till they should recover and come to themselves again; knives had already been drawn several times. For these two days of holiday all this had been torturing me till it made me ill. And indeed I could never endure without repulsion the noise and disorder of drunken people, and especially in this place. On these days even the prison officials did not look into the prison, made no searches, did not look for vodka, understanding that they must allow even these outcasts to enjoy themselves once a year, and that things would be even worse if they did not. At last a sudden fury flamed up in my heart. A political prisoner called M. met me; he looked at me gloomily, his eyes flashed and his lips quivered. 'Je haïs ces brigands!' he hissed to me through his teeth, and walked on. I returned to the prison ward, though only a quarter of an hour before I had rushed out of it, as though I were crazy, when six stalwart fellows had all together flung themselves upon the drunken Tatar Gazin to suppress him and had begun beating him; they beat him stupidly, a camel might have been killed by such blows, but they knew that this Hercules was not easy to kill, and so they beat him without uneasiness. Now on returning I noticed on the bed in the furthest corner of the room Gazin lying unconscious, almost without sign of life. He lay covered with a sheepskin, and every one walked round him, without speaking; though they confidently hoped that he would come to himself next morning, yet if luck was against him, maybe from a beating like that, the man would die. I made my way to my own place opposite the window with the iron grating, and lay on my back with my hands behind my head and my eyes shut. I liked to lie like that; a sleeping man is not molested, and meanwhile one can dream and think. But I could not dream, my heart was beating uneasily, and M.'s words, 'Je haïs ces brigands!' were echoing in my ears. But why describe my impressions; I sometimes dream even now of those times at night, and I have no dreams more agonizing. Perhaps it will be noticed that even to this day I have scarcely once spoken in print of my life in prison. *The House of the Dead* I wrote fifteen years ago in the character of an imaginary person, a criminal who had killed his wife. I may add by the way that since then, very many persons have supposed, and even now maintain, that I was sent to penal servitude for the murder of my wife.

Gradually I sank into forgetfulness and by degrees was lost in memories. During the whole course of my four years in prison I was continually recalling all my past, and seemed to live over again the whole of my life in recollection. These memories rose up of themselves, it was not often that of my own will I summoned them. It would begin from some point, some little thing, at times unnoticed, and then by degrees there would rise up a complete picture, some vivid and complete impression. I used to analyze these impressions, give new features to what had happened long ago, and best of all, I used to correct it, correct it continually, that was my great amusement. On this occasion, I suddenly for some reason remembered an unnoticed moment in my early childhood when I was only nine years old—a moment which I should have thought I had utterly forgotten; but at that time I was particularly fond of memories of my early childhood. I remembered the month of August in our country house: a dry bright day but rather cold and windy; summer was waning and soon we should have to go to Moscow to be bored all the winter over French lessons, and I was so sorry to leave the country. I walked past the threshing-floor and, going down the ravine, I went up to the dense thicket of bushes that covered the further side of the ravine as far as the copse. And I plunged right into the midst of the bushes, and heard a peasant ploughing alone on the clearing about thirty paces away. I knew that he was ploughing up the steep hill and the horse was moving with effort, and from time to time the peasant's call 'come up!' floated upwards to me. I knew almost all our peasants, but I did not know which it was ploughing now, and I did not care who it was, I was absorbed in my own affairs. I was busy, too; I was breaking off switches from the nut trees to whip the frogs with. Nut sticks make such fine whips, but they do not last; while birch twigs are just the opposite. I was interested, too, in beetles and other insects; I used to collect them, some were very ornamental. I was very fond, too, of the little nimble red and yellow lizards with black spots on them, but I was afraid of snakes. Snakes, however, were much more rare than lizards. There were not many mushrooms there. To get mushrooms one had to go to the birch wood, and I was about to set off there. And there was nothing in the world that I loved so much as the wood with its mushrooms and wild berries, with its beetles and its birds, its hedgehogs and squirrels, with its damp smell of dead leaves which I loved so much, and even as I write I smell the fragrance of our birch wood: these impressions will remain for my whole life. Suddenly in the midst of the profound stillness I heard a clear and distinct shout, 'Wolf!' I shrieked and, beside myself with terror, calling out at the top of my voice, ran out into the clearing and straight to the peasant who was ploughing.

It was our peasant Marey. I don't know if there is such a name, but every one called him Marey—a thickset, rather well-grown peasant of fifty, with a good many grey hairs in his dark brown, spreading beard. I knew him, but had scarcely ever happened to speak to him till then. He stopped his horse on hearing my cry, and when, breathless, I caught with one hand at his plough and with the other at his sleeve, he saw how frightened I was.

'There is a wolf!' I cried, panting.

He flung up his head, and could not help looking round for an instant, almost believing me.

'Where is the wolf?'

'A shout...some one shouted: "wolf"...' I faltered out.

'Nonsense, nonsense! A wolf? Why, it was your fancy! How could there be a wolf?' he muttered, reassuring me. But I was trembling all over, and still kept tight hold of his smockfrock, and I must have been quite pale. He looked at me with an uneasy smile, evidently anxious and troubled over me.

'Why, you have had a fright, aïe, aïe!' He shook his head. 'There, dear... Come, little one, aïe!'

He stretched out his hand, and all at once stroked my cheek. 'Come, come, there; Christ be with you! Cross yourself!'

But I did not cross myself. The corners of my mouth were twitching, and I think that struck him particularly. He put out his thick, black-nailed, earth-stained finger and softly touched my twitching lips.

'Aïe, there, there,' he said to me with a slow, almost motherly smile. 'Dear, dear, what is the matter? There; come, come!'

I grasped at last that there was no wolf, and that the shout that I had heard was my fancy. Yet that shout had been so clear and distinct, but such shouts (not only about wolves) I had imagined once or twice before, and I was aware of that. (These hallucinations passed away later as I grew older.)

'Well, I will go then,' I said, looking at him timidly and inquiringly.

'Well, do, and I'll keep watch on you as you go. I won't let the wolf get at you,' he added, still smiling at me with the same motherly expression. 'Well, Christ be with you! Come, run along then,' and he made the sign of the cross over me and then over himself. I walked away, looking back almost at every tenth step. Marey stood still with his mare as I walked away, and looked after me and nodded to me every time I looked round. I must own I felt a little ashamed at having let him see me so frightened, but I was still very much afraid of the wolf as I walked away, until I reached the first barn halfway up the slope of the ravine; there my fright vanished completely, and all at once our yard-dog Voltchok flew to meet me. With Voltchok I felt quite safe, and I turned round to Marey for the last time; I could not see his face distinctly, but I felt that he was still nodding and smiling affectionately to me. I waved to him; he waved back to me and started his little mare. 'Come up!' I heard his call in the distance again, and the little mare pulled at the plough again.

All this I recalled all at once, I don't know why, but with extraordinary minuteness of detail. I suddenly roused myself and sat up on the platform-bed, and, I remember, found myself still smiling quietly at my memories. I brooded over them for another minute.

When I got home that day I told no one of my 'adventure' with Marey. And indeed it was hardly an adventure. And in fact I soon forgot Marey. When I met him now and then afterwards, I never even spoke to him about the wolf or anything else; and all at once now, twenty years afterwards in Siberia, I remembered this meeting with such distinctness to the smallest detail. So it must have lain hidden in my soul, though I knew nothing of it, and rose suddenly to my memory when it was wanted; I remembered the soft motherly smile of the poor serf, the way he signed me with the cross and shook his head. 'There, there, you have had a fright, little one!' And I remembered particularly the thick earth-stained finger with which he softly and with timid tenderness touched my quivering lips. Of course any one would have reassured a child, but something quite different seemed to have happened in that solitary meeting; and if I had been his own son, he could not have looked at me with eyes shining with greater love. And what made him like that? He was our serf and I was his little master, after all. No one would know that he had been kind to me and reward him for it. Was he, perhaps, very fond of little children? Some people are. It was a solitary meeting in the deserted fields, and only God, perhaps, may have seen from above with what deep and humane civilized feeling, and with what delicate, almost feminine tenderness, the heart of a coarse, brutally ignorant Russian serf, who had as yet no expectation, no idea even of his freedom, may be filled. Was not this, perhaps, what Konstantin Aksakov meant when he spoke of the high degree of culture of our peasantry?

And when I got down off the bed and looked around me,

I remember I suddenly felt that I could look at these unhappy creatures with quite different eyes, and that suddenly by some miracle all hatred and anger had vanished utterly from my heart. I walked about, looking into the faces that I met. That shaven peasant, branded on his face as a criminal, bawling his hoarse, drunken song, may be that very Marey; I cannot look into his heart.

I met M. again that evening. Poor fellow! He could have no memories of Russian peasants, and no other view of these people but: 'Je haïs ces brigands!' Yes, the Polish prisoners had more to bear than I.

4

THE CROCODILE:
AN EXTRAORDINARY INCIDENT

A true story of how a gentleman of a certain age and of respectable appearance was swallowed alive by the crocodile in the Arcade, and of the consequences that followed.
Ohé Lambert! Où est Lambert? As tu vu Lambert?

I

On the thirteenth of January of this present year, 1865, at half-past twelve in the day, Elena Ivanovna, the wife of my cultured friend Ivan Matveitch, who is a colleague in the same department, and may be said to be a distant relation of mine, too, expressed the desire to see the crocodile now on view at a fixed charge in the Arcade. As Ivan Matveitch had already in his pocket his ticket for a tour abroad (not so much for the sake of his health as for the improvement of his mind), and was consequently free from his official duties and had nothing whatever to do that morning, he offered no objection to his wife's irresistible fancy, but was positively aflame with curiosity himself.

'A capital idea!' he said, with the utmost satisfaction. 'We'll have a look at the crocodile! On the eve of visiting Europe it is as well to acquaint ourselves on the spot with its indigenous inhabitants.' And with these words, taking his wife's arm, he set off with her at once for the Arcade. I joined them, as I usually do, being an intimate friend of the family. I have never seen Ivan Matveitch in a more agreeable frame of mind than he was on that memorable morning—how true it is that we know not beforehand the fate that awaits us! On entering the Arcade he was at once full of admiration for the splendours of the building, and when we reached the shop in which the monster lately arrived in Petersburg was being exhibited, he volunteered to pay the quarter-rouble for me to the crocodile owner—a thing which had never happened before. Walking into a little room, we observed that besides the crocodile there were in it parrots of the species known as cockatoo, and also a group of monkeys in a special case in a recess. Near the entrance, along the left wall stood a big tin tank that looked like a bath covered with a thin iron grating, filled with water to the depth of two inches. In this shallow pool was kept a huge crocodile, which lay like a log absolutely motionless and apparently deprived of all its faculties by our damp climate, so inhospitable to foreign visitors. This monster at first aroused no special interest in any one of us.

'So this is the crocodile!' said Elena Ivanovna, with a pathetic cadence of regret. 'Why, I thought it was…something different.'

Most probably she thought it was made of diamonds. The owner of the crocodile, a German, came out and looked at us with an air of extraordinary pride.

'He has a right to be,' Ivan Matveitch whispered to me, 'he knows he is the only man in Russia exhibiting a crocodile.'

This quite nonsensical observation I ascribe also to the extremely good-humoured mood which had overtaken Ivan Matveitch, who was on other occasions of rather envious disposition.

'I fancy your crocodile is not alive,' said Elena Ivanovna, piqued by the irresponsive stolidity of the proprietor, and addressing him with a charming smile in order to soften his churlishness—a manoeuvre so typically feminine.

'Oh, no, madam,' the latter replied in broken Russian; and instantly moving the grating half off the tank, he poked the monster's head with a stick.

Then the treacherous monster, to show that it was alive, faintly stirred its paws and tail, raised its snout and emitted something like a prolonged snuffle.

'Come, don't be cross, Karlchen,' said the German caressingly, gratified in his vanity.

'How horrid that crocodile is! I am really frightened,' Elena Ivanovna twittered, still more coquettishly. 'I know I shall dream of him now.'

'But he won't bite you if you do dream of him,' the German retorted gallantly, and was the first to laugh at his own jest, but none of us responded.

'Come, Semyon Semyonitch,' said Elena Ivanovna, addressing me exclusively, 'let us go and look at the monkeys. I am awfully fond of monkeys; they are such darlings...and the crocodile is horrid.'

'Oh, don't be afraid, my dear!' Ivan Matveitch called after us, gallantly displaying his manly courage to his wife. 'This drowsy denison of the realms of the Pharaohs will do us no harm.' And he remained by the tank. What is more, he took his glove and began tickling the crocodile's nose with it, wishing, as he said afterwards, to induce him to snort. The proprietor showed his politeness to a lady by following Elena Ivanovna to the case of monkeys.

So everything was going well, and nothing could have been foreseen. Elena Ivanovna was quite skittish in her raptures over the monkeys, and seemed completely taken up with them.

With shrieks of delight she was continually turning to me, as though determined not to notice the proprietor, and kept gushing with laughter at the resemblance she detected between these monkeys and her intimate friends and acquaintances. I, too, was amused, for the resemblance was unmistakable. The German did not know whether to laugh or not, and so at last was reduced to frowning. And it was at that moment that a terrible, I may say unnatural, scream set the room vibrating. Not knowing what to think, for the first moment I stood still, numb with horror, but noticing that Elena Ivanovna was screaming too, I quickly turned round—and what did I behold! I saw—oh, heavens!—I saw the luckless Ivan Matveitch in the terrible jaws of the crocodile, held by them round the waist, lifted horizontally in the air and desperately kicking. Then—one moment, and no trace remained of him. But I must describe it in detail, for I stood all the while motionless, and had time to watch the whole process taking place before me with an attention and interest such as I never remember to have felt before. 'What,' I thought at that critical moment, 'what if all that had happened to me instead of to Ivan Matveitch—how unpleasant it would have been for me!'

But to return to my story. The crocodile began by turning the unhappy Ivan Matveitch in his terrible jaws so that he could swallow his legs first; then bringing up Ivan Matveitch, who kept trying to jump out and clutching at the sides of the tank, sucked him down again as far as his waist. Then bringing him up again, gulped him down, and so again and again. In this way Ivan Matveitch was visibly disappearing before our eyes. At last, with a final gulp, the crocodile swallowed my cultured friend entirely, this time leaving no trace of him. From the outside of the crocodile we could see the protuberances of Ivan Matveitch's figure as he passed down the inside of the monster. I was on the point of screaming again when destiny played another treacherous trick upon us. The crocodile made a tremendous effort, probably oppressed by the magnitude of the object he had swallowed, once more opened his terrible jaws, and with a final hiccup he suddenly let the head of Ivan Matveitch pop out for a second, with an expression of despair on his face. In that brief instant the spectacles dropped off his nose to the bottom of the tank. It seemed as though that despairing countenance had only popped out to cast one last look on the objects around it, to take its last farewell of all earthly pleasures. But it had not time to carry out its intention; the crocodile made another effort, gave a gulp and instantly it vanished again—this time for ever. This appearance and disappearance of a still living human head was so horrible, but at the same—either from its rapidity and unexpectedness or from the dropping of the spectacles—there was something so comic about it that I suddenly quite unexpectedly exploded with laughter. But pulling myself together and realizing that to laugh at such a moment was not the thing for an old family friend, I turned at once to Elena Ivanovna and said with a sympathetic air:

'Now it's all over with our friend Ivan Matveitch!'

I cannot even attempt to describe how violent was the agitation of Elena Ivanovna during the whole process. After the first scream she seemed rooted to the spot, and stared at the catastrophe with apparent indifference, though her eyes looked as though they were starting out of her head; then she suddenly went off into a heart-rending wail, but I seized her hands. At this instant the proprietor, too, who had at first been also petrified by horror, suddenly clasped his hands and cried, gazing upwards:

'Oh my crocodile! Oh mein allerliebster Karlchen! Mutter, Mutter, Mutter!'

A door at the rear of the room opened at this cry, and the

Mutter, a rosy-cheeked, elderly but dishevelled woman in a cap made her appearance, and rushed with a shriek to her German.

A perfect Bedlam followed. Elena Ivanovna kept shrieking out the same phrase, as though in a frenzy, 'Flay him! Flay him!' apparently entreating them—probably in a moment of oblivion—to flay somebody for something. The proprietor and Mutter took no notice whatever of either of us; they were both bellowing like calves over the crocodile.

'He did for himself! He will burst himself at once, for he did swallow a ganz official!' cried the proprietor.

'Unser Karlchen, unser allerliebster Karlchen wird sterben,' howled his wife.

'We are bereaved and without bread!' chimed in the proprietor.

'Flay him! Flay him! Flay him!' clamoured Elena Ivanovna, clutching at the German's coat.

'He did tease the crocodile. For what did your man tease the crocodile?' cried the German, pulling away from her. 'You will if Karlchen wird burst, therefore pay, das war mein Sohn, das war mein einziger Sohn.'

I must own I was intensely indignant at the sight of such egoism in the German and the cold-heartedness of his dishevelled Mutter; at the same time Elena Ivanovna's reiterated shriek of 'Flay him! Flay him!' troubled me even more and absorbed at last my whole attention, positively alarming me. I may as well say straight off that I entirely misunderstood this strange exclamation: it seemed to me that Elena Ivanovna had for the moment taken leave of her senses, but nevertheless wishing to avenge the loss of her beloved Ivan Matveitch, was demanding by way of compensation that the crocodile should be severely thrashed, while she was meaning something quite different. Looking round at the door, not without embarrassment, I began to entreat Elena Ivanovna to calm herself, and above all not to use the shocking word 'flay'. For such a reactionary desire here, in the midst of the Arcade and of the most cultured society, not two paces from the hall where at this very minute Mr Lavrov was perhaps delivering a public lecture, was not only impossible but unthinkable, and might at any moment bring upon us the hisses of culture and the caricatures of Mr Stepanov. To my horror I was immediately proved to be correct in my alarmed suspicions: the curtain that divided the crocodile room from the little entry where the quarter-roubles were taken suddenly parted, and in the opening there appeared a figure with moustaches and beard, carrying a cap, with the upper part of its body bent a long way forward, though the feet were scrupulously held beyond the threshold of the crocodile room in order to avoid the necessity of paying the entrance money.

'Such a reactionary desire, madam,' said the stranger, trying to avoid falling over in our direction and to remain standing outside the room, 'does no credit to your development, and is conditioned by lack of phosphorus in your brain. You will be promptly held up to shame in the *Chronicle of Progress* and in our satirical prints...'

But he could not complete his remarks; the proprietor coming to himself, and seeing with horror that a man was talking in the crocodile room without having paid entrance money, rushed furiously at the progressive stranger and turned him out with a punch from each fist. For a moment both vanished from our sight behind a curtain, and only then I grasped that the whole uproar was about nothing. Elena Ivanovna turned out quite innocent; she had, as I have mentioned already, no idea whatever of subjecting the crocodile to a degrading corporal punishment, and had simply expressed the desire that he should be opened and her husband released from his interior.

'What! You wish that my crocodile be perished!' the

proprietor yelled, running in again. 'No! let your husband be perished first, before my crocodile!... Mein Vater showed crocodile, mein Grossvater showed crocodile, mein Sohn will show crocodile, and I will show crocodile! All will show crocodile! I am known to ganz Europa, and you are not known to ganz Europa, and you must pay me a strafe!'

'Ja, ja,' put in the vindictive German woman, 'we shall not let you go. Strafe, since Karlchen is burst!'

'And, indeed, it's useless to flay the creature,' I added calmly, anxious to get Elena Ivanovna away home as quickly as possible, 'as our dear Ivan Matveitch is by now probably soaring somewhere in the empyrean.'

'My dear'—we suddenly heard, to our intense amazement, the voice of Ivan Matveitch—'my dear, my advice is to apply direct to the superintendent's office, as without the assistance of the police the German will never be made to see reason.'

These words, uttered with firmness and aplomb, and expressing an exceptional presence of mind, for the first minute so astounded us that we could not believe our ears. But, of course, we ran at once to the crocodile's tank, and with equal reverence and incredulity listened to the unhappy captive. His voice was muffled, thin and even squeaky, as though it came from a considerable distance. It reminded one of a jocose person who, covering his mouth with a pillow, shouts from an adjoining room, trying to mimic the sound of two peasants calling to one another in a deserted plain or across a wide ravine—a performance to which I once had the pleasure of listening in a friend's house at Christmas.

'Ivan Matveitch, my dear, and so you are alive!' faltered Elena Ivanovna.

'Alive and well,' answered Ivan Matveitch, 'and, thanks to the Almighty, swallowed without any damage whatever. I am only uneasy as to the view my superiors may take of the incident; for after getting a permit to go abroad I've got into a crocodile, which seems anything but clever.'

'But, my dear, don't trouble your head about being clever; first of all we must somehow excavate you from where you are,' Elena Ivanovna interrupted.

'Excavate!' cried the proprietor. 'I will not let my crocodile be excavated. Now the publicum will come many more, and I will fünfzig kopecks ask and Karlchen will cease to burst.'

'Gott sei dank!' put in his wife.

'They are right,' Ivan Matveitch observed tranquilly; 'the principles of economics before everything.'

'My dear! I will fly at once to the authorities and lodge a complaint, for I feel that we cannot settle this mess by ourselves.'

'I think so too,' observed Ivan Matveitch; 'but in our age of industrial crisis it is not easy to rip open the belly of a crocodile without economic compensation, and meanwhile the inevitable question presents itself: What will the German take for his crocodile? And with it another: How will it be paid? For, as you know, I have no means...'

'Perhaps out of your salary...' I observed timidly, but the proprietor interrupted me at once.

'I will not the crocodile sell; I will for three thousand the crocodile sell! I will for four thousand the crocodile sell! Now the publicum will come very many. I will for five thousand the crocodile sell!'

In fact he gave himself insufferable airs. Covetousness and a revolting greed gleamed joyfully in his eyes.

'I am going!' I cried indignantly.

'And I! I too! I shall go to Andrey Osipitch himself. I will soften him with my tears,' whined Elena Ivanovna.

'Don't do that, my dear,' Ivan Matveitch hastened to interpose. He had long been jealous of Andrey Osipitch on his wife's account, and he knew she would enjoy going to weep before a gentleman of refinement, for tears suited her. 'And I don't advise you to do so either, my friend,' he added, addressing me. 'It's no good plunging headlong in that slapdash way; there's no knowing what it may lead to. You had much better go today to Timofey Semyonitch, as though to pay an ordinary visit; he is an old-fashioned and by no means brilliant man, but he is trustworthy, and what matters most of all, he is straightforward. Give him my greetings and describe the circumstances of the case. And since I owe him seven roubles over our last game of cards, take the opportunity to pay him the money; that will soften the stern old man. In any case his advice may serve as a guide for us. And meanwhile take Elena Ivanovna home... Calm yourself, my dear,' he continued, addressing her. 'I am weary of these outcries and feminine squabblings, and should like a nap. It's soft and warm in here, though I have hardly had time to look round in this unexpected haven.'

'Look round! Why, is it light in there?' cried Elena Ivanovna in a tone of relief.

'I am surrounded by impenetrable night,' answered the poor captive; 'but I can feel and, so to speak, have a look round with my hands... Good-bye; set your mind at rest and don't deny yourself recreation and diversion. Till tomorrow! And you, Semyon Semyonitch, come to me in the evening, and as you are absent-minded and may forget it, tie a knot in your handkerchief.'

I confess I was glad to get away, for I was overtired and somewhat bored. Hastening to offer my arm to the disconsolate Elena Ivanovna, whose charms were only enhanced by her agitation, I hurriedly led her out of the crocodile room.

'The charge will be another quarter-rouble in the evening,' the proprietor called after us.

'Oh, dear, how greedy they are!' said Elena Ivanovna, looking at herself in every mirror on the walls of the Arcade, and evidently aware that she was looking prettier than usual.

'The principles of economics,' I answered with some emotion, proud that passers-by should see the lady on my arm.

'The principles of economics,' she drawled in a touching little voice. 'I did not in the least understand what Ivan Matveitch said about those horrid economics just now.'

'I will explain to you,' I answered, and began at once telling her of the beneficial effects of the introduction of foreign capital into our country, upon which I had read an article in the *Petersburg News* and the *Voice* that morning.

'How strange it is,' she interrupted, after listening for some time. 'But do leave off, you horrid man. What nonsense you are talking... Tell me, do I look purple?'

'You look perfect, and not purple!' I observed, seizing the opportunity to pay her a compliment.

'Naughty man!' she said complacently. 'Poor Ivan Matveitch,' she added a minute later, putting her little head on one side coquettishly. 'I am really sorry for him. Oh, dear!' she cried suddenly, 'how is he going to have his dinner...and... and...what will he do...if he wants anything?'

'An unforeseen question,' I answered, perplexed in my turn. To tell the truth, it had not entered my head, so much more practical are women than we men in the solution of the problems of daily life!

'Poor dear! how could he have got into such a mess... nothing to amuse him, and in the dark... How vexing it is that I have no photograph of him... And so now I am a sort of widow,' she added, with a seductive smile, evidently interested in her new position. 'Hm!... I am sorry for him, though.'

It was, in short, the expression of the very natural and intelligible grief of a young and interesting wife for the loss of her husband. I took her home at last, soothed her, and after dining with her and drinking a cup of aromatic coffee, set off at six o'clock to Timofey Semyonitch, calculating that at that hour all married people of settled habits would be sitting or lying down at home.

Having written this first chapter in a style appropriate to the incident recorded, I intend to proceed in a language more natural though less elevated, and I beg to forewarn the reader of the fact.

II

The venerable Timofey Semyonitch met me rather nervously, as though somewhat embarrassed. He led me to his tiny study and shut the door carefully, 'that the children may not hinder us,' he added with evident uneasiness. There he made me sit down on a chair by the writing-table, sat down himself in an easy chair, wrapped round him the skirts of his old wadded dressing-gown, and assumed an official and even severe air, in readiness for anything, though he was not my chief nor Ivan Matveitch's, and had hitherto been reckoned as a colleague and even a friend.

'First of all,' he said, 'take note that I am not a person in authority, but just such a subordinate official as you and Ivan Matveitch… I have nothing to do with it, and do not intend to mix myself up in the affair.'

I was surprised to find that he apparently knew all about it already. In spite of that I told him the whole story over in detail. I spoke with positive excitement, for I was at that moment fulfilling the obligations of a true friend. He listened without special surprise, but with evident signs of suspicion.

'Only fancy,' he said, 'I always believed that this would be sure to happen to him.'

'Why, Timofey Semyonitch? It is a very unusual incident in itself…'

'I admit it. But Ivan Matveitch's whole career in the service was leading up to this end. He was flighty—conceited indeed. It was always "progress" and ideas of all sorts, and this is what progress brings people to!'

'But this is a most unusual incident and cannot possibly serve as a general rule for all progressives.'

'Yes, indeed it can. You see, it's the effect of over-education, I assure you. For over-education leads people to poke their noses into all sorts of places, especially where they are not invited. Though perhaps you know best,' he added, as though offended. 'I am an old man and not of much education. I began as a soldier's son, and this year has been the jubilee of my service.'

'Oh, no, Timofey Semyonitch, not at all. On the contrary, Ivan Matveitch is eager for your advice; he is eager for your guidance. He implores it, so to say, with tears.'

'So to say, with tears! Hm! Those are crocodile's tears and one cannot quite believe in them. Tell me, what possessed him to want to go abroad? And how could he afford to go? Why, he has no private means!'

'He had saved the money from his last bonus,' I answered plaintively. 'He only wanted to go for three months—to Switzerland...to the land of William Tell.'

'William Tell? Hm!'

'He wanted to meet the spring at Naples, to see the museums, the customs, the animals...'

'Hm! The animals! I think it was simply from pride. What animals? Animals, indeed! Haven't we animals enough? We have museums, menageries, camels. There are bears quite close to Petersburg! And here he's got inside a crocodile himself...'

'Oh, come, Timofey Semyonitch! The man is in trouble, the man appeals to you as to a friend, as to an older relation, craves for advice—and you reproach him. Have pity at least on the unfortunate Elena Ivanovna!'

'You are speaking of his wife? A charming little lady,' said Timofey Semyonitch, visibly softening and taking a pinch of snuff with relish. 'Particularly prepossessing. And so plump, and always putting her pretty little head on one side... Very agreeable. Andrey Osipitch was speaking of her only the other day.'

'Speaking of her?'

'Yes, and in very flattering terms. Such a bust, he said, such eyes, such hair... A sugar-plum, he said, not a lady—and then he laughed. He is still a young man, of course.' Timofey Semyonitch blew his nose with a loud noise. 'And yet, young though he is, what a career he is making for himself.'

'That's quite a different thing, Timofey Semyonitch.'

'Of course, of course.'

'Well, what do you say then, Timofey Semyonitch?'

'Why, what can I do?'

'Give advice, guidance, as a man of experience, a relative! What are we to do? What steps are we to take? Go to the authorities and...'

'To the authorities? Certainly not,' Timofey Semyonitch replied hurriedly. 'If you ask my advice, you had better, above all, hush the matter up and act, so to speak, as a private person. It is a suspicious incident, quite unheard of. Unheard of, above all; there is no precedent for it, and it is far from creditable... And so discretion above all... Let him lie there a bit. We must wait and see...'

'But how can we wait and see, Timofey Semyonitch? What if he is stifled there?'

'Why should he be? I think you told me that he made himself fairly comfortable there?'

I told him the whole story over again. Timofey Semyonitch pondered.

'Hm!' he said, twisting his snuffbox in his hands. 'To my

mind it's really a good thing he should lie there a bit, instead of going abroad. Let him reflect at his leisure. Of course he mustn't be stifled, and so he must take measures to preserve his health, avoiding a cough, for instance, and so on... And as for the German, it's my personal opinion he is within his rights, and even more so than the other side, because it was the other party who got into *his* crocodile without asking permission, and not *he* who got into Ivan Matveitch's crocodile without asking permission, though, so far as I recollect, the latter has no crocodile. And a crocodile is private property, and so it is impossible to slit him open without compensation.'

'For the saving of human life, Timofey Semyonitch.'

'Oh, well, that's a matter for the police. You must go to them.'

'But Ivan Matveitch may be needed in the department. He may be asked for.'

'Ivan Matveitch needed? Ha-ha! Besides, he is on leave, so that we may ignore him—let him inspect the countries of Europe! It will be a different matter if he doesn't turn up when his leave is over. Then we shall ask for him and make inquiries.'

'Three months! Timofey Semyonitch, for pity's sake!'

'It's his own fault. Nobody thrust him there. At this rate we should have to get a nurse to look after him at government expense, and that is not allowed for in the regulations. But the chief point is that the crocodile is private property, so that the principles of economics apply in this question. And the principles of economics are paramount. Only the other evening, at Luka Andreitch's, Ignaty Prokofyitch was saying so. Do you know Ignaty Prokofyitch? A capitalist, in a big way of business, and he speaks so fluently. "We need industrial development," he said; "there is very little development among us. We must create it. We must create capital, so we must create a middle-class, the so-called bourgeoisie. And as we haven't capital we must attract it from abroad. We must, in the first place, give facilities to foreign companies to buy up lands in Russia as is done now abroad. The communal holding of land is poison, is ruin." And, you know, he spoke with such heat; well, that's all right for him—a wealthy man, and not in the service. "With the communal system," he said, "there will be no improvement in industrial development or agriculture. Foreign companies," he said, "must as far as possible buy up the whole of our land in big lots, and then split it up, split it up, split it up, in the smallest parts possible"—and do you know he pronounced the words "split it up" with such determination—"and then sell it as private property. Or rather, not sell it, but simply let it. When," he said, "all the land is in the hands of foreign companies they can fix any rent they like. And so the peasant will work three times as much for his daily bread and he can be turned out at pleasure. So that he will feel it, will be submissive and industrious, and will work three times as much for the same wages. But as it is, with the commune, what does he care? He knows he won't die of hunger, so he is lazy and drunken. And meanwhile money will be attracted into Russia, capital will be created and the bourgeoisie will spring up. The English political and literary paper, *The Times*, in an article the other day on our finances stated that the reason our financial position was so unsatisfactory was that we had no middle-class, no big fortunes, no accommodating proletariat." Ignaty Prokofyitch speaks well. He is an orator. He wants to lay a report on the subject before the authorities, and then to get it published in the *News*. That's something very different from verses like Ivan Matveitch's...'

'But how about Ivan Matveitch?' I put in, after letting the old man babble on.

Timofey Semyonitch was sometimes fond of talking and showing that he was not behind the times, but knew all about things.

'How about Ivan Matveitch? Why, I am coming to that. Here we are, anxious to bring foreign capital into the country—and only consider: as soon as the capital of a foreigner, who has been attracted to Petersburg, has been doubled through Ivan Matveitch, instead of protecting the foreign capitalist, we are proposing to rip open the belly of his original capital—the crocodile. Is it consistent? To my mind, Ivan Matveitch, as the true son of his fatherland, ought to rejoice and to be proud that through him the value of a foreign crocodile has been doubled and possibly even trebled. That's just what is wanted to attract capital. If one man succeeds, mind you, another will come with a crocodile, and a third will bring two or three of them at once, and capital will grow up about them—there you have a bourgeoisie. It must be encouraged.'

'Upon my word, Timofey Semyonitch!' I cried, 'you are demanding almost supernatural self-sacrifice from poor Ivan Matveitch.'

'I demand nothing, and I beg you, before everything—as I have said already—to remember that I am not a person in authority and so cannot demand anything of any one. I am speaking as a son of the fatherland, that is, not as the *Son of the Fatherland*, but as a son of the fatherland. Again, what possessed him to get into the crocodile? A respectable man, a man of good grade in the service, lawfully married—and then to behave like that! Is it consistent?'

'But it was an accident.'

'Who knows? And where is the money to compensate the owner to come from?'

'Perhaps out of his salary, Timofey Semyonitch?'

'Would that be enough?'

'No, it wouldn't, Timofey Semyonitch,' I answered sadly. 'The proprietor was at first alarmed that the crocodile would burst, but as soon as he was sure that it was all right, he began to bluster and was delighted to think that he could double the charge for entry.'

'Treble and quadruple perhaps! The public will simply stampede the place now, and crocodile owners are smart people. Besides, it's not Lent yet, and people are keen on diversions, and so I say again, the great thing is that Ivan Matveitch should preserve his incognito, don't let him be in a hurry. Let everybody know, perhaps, that he is in the crocodile, but don't let them be officially informed of it. Ivan Matveitch is in particularly favourable circumstances for that, for he is reckoned to be abroad. It will be said he is in the crocodile, and we will refuse to believe it. That is how it can be managed. The great thing is that he should wait; and why should he be in a hurry?'

'Well, but if...'

'Don't worry, he has a good constitution...'

'Well, and afterwards, when he has waited?'

'Well, I won't conceal from you that the case is exceptional in the highest degree. One doesn't know what to think of it, and the worst of it is there is no precedent. If we had a precedent we might have something to go by. But as it is, what is one to say? It will certainly take time to settle it.'

A happy thought flashed upon my mind.

'Cannot we arrange,' I said, 'that if he is destined to remain in the entrails of the monster and it is the will of Providence that he should remain alive, that he should send in a petition to be reckoned as still serving?'

'Hm!... Possibly as on leave and without salary...'

'But couldn't it be with salary?'

'On what grounds?'

'As sent on a special commission.'

'What commission and where?'

'Why, into the entrails, the entrails of the crocodile... So to speak, for exploration, for investigation of the facts on the spot. It would, of course, be a novelty, but that is progressive and would at the same time show zeal for enlightenment.'

Timofey Semyonitch thought a little.

'To send a special official,' he said at last, 'to the inside of a crocodile to conduct a special inquiry is, in my personal opinion, an absurdity. It is not in the regulations. And what sort of special inquiry could there be there?'

'The scientific study of nature on the spot, in the living subject. The natural sciences are all the fashion nowadays, botany... He could live there and report his observations... For instance, concerning digestion or simply habits. For the sake of accumulating facts.'

'You mean as statistics. Well, I am no great authority on that subject, indeed I am no philosopher at all. You say "facts"— we are overwhelmed with facts as it is, and don't know what to do with them. Besides, statistics are a danger.'

'In what way?'

'They are a danger. Moreover, you will admit he will report facts, so to speak, lying like a log. And, can one do one's official duties lying like a log? That would be another novelty and a dangerous one; and again, there is no precedent for it. If we had any sort of precedent for it, then, to my thinking, he might have been given the job.'

'But no live crocodiles have been brought over hitherto, Timofey Semyonitch.'

'Hm...yes,' he reflected again. 'Your objection is a just one, if you like, and might indeed serve as a ground for carrying the matter further; but consider again, that if with the arrival of living crocodiles government clerks begin to disappear, and then on the ground that they are warm and comfortable there, expect to receive the official sanction for their position, and then take their ease there...you must admit it would be a bad example. We should have every one trying to go the same way to get a salary for nothing.'

'Do your best for him, Timofey Semyonitch. By the way, Ivan Matveitch asked me to give you seven roubles he had lost to you at cards.'

'Ah, he lost that the other day at Nikifor Nikiforitch's. I remember. And how gay and amusing he was—and now!'

The old man was genuinely touched.

'Intercede for him, Timofey Semyonitch!'

'I will do my best. I will speak in my own name, as a private person, as though I were asking for information. And meanwhile, you find out indirectly, unofficially, how much would the proprietor consent to take for his crocodile?'

Timofey Semyonitch was visibly more friendly.

'Certainly,' I answered. 'And I will come back to you at once to report.'

'And his wife...is she alone now? Is she depressed?'

'You should call on her, Timofey Semyonitch.'

'I will. I thought of doing so before; it's a good opportunity... And what on earth possessed him to go and look at the crocodile? Though, indeed, I should like to see it myself.'

'Go and see the poor fellow, Timofey Semyonitch.'

'I will. Of course, I don't want to raise his hopes by doing so. I shall go as a private person... Well, good-bye, I am going to Nikifor Nikiforitch's again: shall you be there?'

'No, I am going to see the poor prisoner.'

'Yes, now he is a prisoner!... Ah, that's what comes of thoughtlessness!'

I said good-bye to the old man. Ideas of all kinds were straying through my mind. A good-natured and most honest man, Timofey Semyonitch, yet, as I left him, I felt pleased at the thought that he had celebrated his fiftieth year of service, and that Timofey Semyonitchs are now a rarity among us. I flew at once, of course, to the Arcade to tell poor Ivan Matveitch all the news. And, indeed, I was moved by curiosity to know how he was getting on in the crocodile and how it was possible to live in a crocodile. And, indeed, was it possible to live in a crocodile at all? At times it really seemed to me as though it were all an outlandish, monstrous dream, especially as an outlandish monster was the chief figure in it.

III

And yet it was not a dream, but actual, indubitable fact. Should I be telling the story if it were not? But to continue.

It was late, about nine o'clock, before I reached the Arcade, and I had to go into the crocodile room by the back entrance, for the German had closed the shop earlier than usual that evening. Now in the seclusion of domesticity he was walking about in a greasy old frock-coat, but he seemed three times as pleased as he had been in the morning. It was evidently that he had no apprehensions now, and that the public had been coming 'many more'. The Mutter came out later, evidently to keep an eye on me. The German and the Mutter frequently whispered together. Although the shop was closed he charged me a quarter-rouble! What unnecessary exactitude!

'You will every time pay; the public will one rouble, and you one quarter pay; for you are the good friend of your good friend; and I a friend respect...'

'Are you alive, are you alive, my cultured friend?' I cried, as I approached the crocodile, expecting my words to reach Ivan Matveitch from a distance and to flatter his vanity.

'Alive and well,' he answered, as though from a long way off or from under the bed, though I was standing close beside him. 'Alive and well; but of that later... How are things going?'

As though purposely not hearing the question, I was just beginning with sympathetic haste to question him how he was, what it was like in the crocodile, and what, in fact, there was inside a crocodile. Both friendship and common civility demanded this. But with capricious annoyance he interrupted me.

'How are things going?' he shouted, in a shrill and on this occasion particularly revolting voice, addressing me peremptorily as usual.

I described to him my whole conversation with Timofey Semyonitch down to the smallest detail. As I told my story I tried to show my resentment in my voice.

'The old man is right,' Ivan Matveitch pronounced as abruptly as usual in his conversation with me. 'I like practical people, and can't endure sentimental milksops. I am ready to admit, however, that your idea about a special commission is not altogether absurd. I certainly have a great deal to report, both from a scientific and from an ethical point of view. But now all this has taken a new and unexpected aspect, and it is not worth while to trouble about mere salary. Listen attentively. Are you sitting down?'

'No, I am standing up.'

'Sit down on the floor if there is nothing else, and listen attentively.'

Resentfully I took a chair and put it down on the floor with a bang, in my anger.

'Listen,' he began dictatorially. 'The public came today in masses. There was no room left in the evening, and the police came in to keep order. At eight o'clock, that is, earlier than usual, the proprietor thought it necessary to close the shop and end the exhibition to count the money he had taken and prepare for tomorrow more conveniently. So I know there will be a regular fair tomorrow. So we may assume that all the most cultivated people in the capital, the ladies of the best society, the foreign ambassadors, the leading lawyers and so on, will all be present. What's more, people will be flowing here from the remotest provinces of our vast and interesting empire. The upshot of it is that I am the cynosure of all eyes, and though hidden to sight, I am eminent. I shall teach the idle crowd. Taught by experience, I shall be an example of greatness and resignation to fate! I shall be, so to say, a pulpit from which to instruct mankind. The mere biological details I can furnish about the monster I am inhabiting are of priceless value. And so, far from repining at what has happened, I confidently hope for the most brilliant of careers.'

'You won't find it wearisome?' I asked sarcastically.

What irritated me more than anything was the extreme pomposity of his language. Nevertheless, it all rather disconcerted me. 'What on earth, what, can this frivolous blockhead find to be so cocky about?' I muttered to myself. 'He ought to be crying instead of being cocky.'

'No!' he answered my observation sharply, 'for I am full of great ideas, only now can I at leisure ponder over the amelioration of the lot of humanity. Truth and light will come forth now from the crocodile. I shall certainly develop a new economic theory of my own and I shall be proud of it—which I have hitherto been prevented from doing by my official duties and by trivial distractions. I shall refute everything and be a new Fourier. By the way, did you give Timofey Semyonitch the seven roubles?'

'Yes, out of my own pocket,' I answered, trying to emphasize that fact in my voice.

'We will settle it,' he answered superciliously. 'I confidently expect my salary to be raised, for who should get a raise if not I? I am of the utmost service now. But to business. My wife?'

'You are, I suppose, inquiring after Elena Ivanovna?'

'My wife?' he shouted, this time in a positive squeal.

There was no help for it! Meekly, though gnashing my

teeth, I told him how I had left Elena Ivanovna. He did not even hear me out.

'I have special plans in regard to her,' he began impatiently. 'If I am celebrated *here*, I wish her to be celebrated *there*. Savants, poets, philosophers, foreign mineralogists, statesmen, after conversing in the morning with me, will visit her salon in the evening. From next week onwards she must have an "At Home" every evening. With my salary doubled, we shall have the means for entertaining, and as the entertainment must not go beyond tea and hired footmen—that's settled. Both here and there they will talk of me. I have long thirsted for an opportunity for being talked about, but could not attain it, fettered by my humble position and low grade in the service. And now all this has been attained by a simple gulp on the part of the crocodile. Every word of mine will be listened to, every utterance will be thought over, repeated, printed. And I'll teach them what I am worth! They shall understand at last what abilities they have allowed to vanish in the entrails of a monster. "This man might have been Foreign Minister or might have ruled a kingdom," some will say. "And that man did not rule a kingdom," others will say. In what way am I inferior to a Garnier-Pagesishky or whatever they are called? My wife must be a worthy second—I have brains, she has beauty and charm. "She is beautiful, and that is why she is his wife," some will say. "She is beautiful *because* she is his wife," others will amend. To be ready for anything let Elena Ivanovna buy tomorrow the Encyclopædia edited by Andrey Kraevsky, that she may be able to converse on any topic. Above all, let her be sure to read the political leader in the *Petersburg News*, comparing it every day with the *Voice*. I imagine that the proprietor will consent to take me sometimes with the crocodile to my wife's brilliant salon. I will be in a tank in the middle of the magnificent drawing-room, and I will scintillate with witticisms which I will prepare in the morning. To the statesmen I will impart my projects; to the poet I will speak in rhyme; with the ladies I can be amusing and charming without impropriety, since I shall be no danger to their husbands' peace of mind. To all the rest I shall serve as a pattern of resignation to fate and the will of Providence. I shall make my wife a brilliant literary lady; I shall bring her forward and explain her to the public; as my wife she must be full of the most striking virtues; and if they are right in calling Andrey Alexandrovitch our Russian Alfred de Musset, they will be still more right in calling her our Russian Yevgenia Tour.'

I must confess that although this wild nonsense was rather in Ivan Matveitch's habitual style, it did occur to me that he was in a fever and delirious. It was the same, everyday Ivan Matveitch, but magnified twenty times.

'My friend,' I asked him, 'are you hoping for a long life? Tell me, in fact, are you well? How do you eat, how do you sleep, how do you breathe? I am your friend, and you must admit that the incident is most unnatural, and consequently my curiosity is most natural.'

'Idle curiosity and nothing else,' he pronounced sententiously, 'but you shall be satisfied. You ask how I am managing in the entrails of the monster? To begin with, the crocodile, to my amusement, turns out to be perfectly empty. His inside consists of a sort of huge empty sack made of gutta-percha, like the elastic goods sold in the Gorohovy Street, in the Morskaya, and, if I am not mistaken, in the Voznesensky Prospect. Otherwise, if you think of it, how could I find room?'

'Is it possible?' I cried, in a surprise that may well be understood. 'Can the crocodile be perfectly empty?'

'Perfectly,' Ivan Matveitch maintained sternly and impressively. 'And in all probability, it is so constructed by the laws of Nature. The crocodile possesses nothing but jaws furnished with sharp teeth, and besides the jaws, a tail of considerable length—that is all, properly speaking. The middle part between these two extremities is an empty space enclosed by something of the nature of gutta-percha, probably really gutta-percha.'

'But the ribs, the stomach, the intestines, the liver, the heart?' I interrupted quite angrily.

'There is nothing, absolutely nothing of all that, and probably there never has been. All that is the idle fancy of frivolous travellers. As one inflates an air-cushion, I am now with my person inflating the crocodile. He is incredibly elastic. Indeed, you might, as the friend of the family, get in with me if you were generous and self-sacrificing enough—and even with you here there would be room to spare. I even think that in the last resort I might send for Elena Ivanovna. However, this void, hollow formation of the crocodile is quite in keeping with the teachings of natural science. If, for instance, one had to construct a new crocodile, the question would naturally present itself. What is the fundamental characteristic of the crocodile? The answer is clear: to swallow human beings. How is one, in constructing the crocodile, to secure that he should swallow people? The answer is clearer still: construct him hollow. It was settled by physics long ago that Nature abhors a vacuum. Hence the inside of the crocodile must be hollow so that it may abhor the vacuum, and consequently swallow and so fill itself with anything it can come across. And that is the sole rational cause why every crocodile swallows men. It is not the same in the constitution of man: the emptier a man's head is, for instance, the less he feels the thirst to fill it, and that is the one exception to the general rule. It is all as clear as day to me now. I have deduced it by my own observation and experience, being, so to say, in the very bowels of Nature, in its retort, listening to the throbbing of its pulse. Even etymology supports me, for the very word crocodile means voracity. Crocodile—

crocodillo—is evidently an Italian word, dating perhaps from the Egyptian Pharaohs, and evidently derived from the French verb croquer, which means to eat, to devour, in general to absorb nourishment. All these remarks I intend to deliver as my first lecture in Elena Ivanovna's salon when they take me there in the tank.'

'My friend, oughtn't you at least to take some purgative?' I cried involuntarily.

'He is in a fever, a fever, he is feverish!' I repeated to myself in alarm.

'Nonsense!' he answered contemptuously. 'Besides, in my present position it would be most inconvenient. I knew, though, you would be sure to talk of taking medicine.'

'But, my friend, how…how do you take food now? Have you dined today?'

'No, but I am not hungry, and most likely I shall never take food again. And that, too, is quite natural; filling the whole interior of the crocodile I make him feel always full. Now he need not be fed for some years. On the other hand, nourished by me, he will naturally impart to me all the vital juices of his body; it is the same as with some accomplished coquettes who embed themselves and their whole persons for the night in raw steak, and then, after their morning bath, are fresh, supple, buxom and fascinating. In that way nourishing the crocodile, I myself obtain nourishment from him, consequently we mutually nourish one another. But as it is difficult even for a crocodile to digest a man like me, he must, no doubt, be conscious of a certain weight in his stomach—an organ which he does not, however, possess—and that is why, to avoid causing the creature suffering, I do not often turn over, and although I could turn over I do not do so from humanitarian motives. This is the one drawback of my present position, and in an allegorical sense Timofey Semyonitch was right in saying I was lying like a log. But I will prove that even lying like a log—nay, that only lying like a log—one can revolutionize the lot of mankind. All the great ideas and movements of our newspapers and magazines have evidently been the work of men who were lying like logs; that is why they call them divorced from the realities of life—but what does it matter, their saying that! I am constructing now a complete system of my own, and you wouldn't believe how easy it is! You have only to creep into a secluded corner or into a crocodile, to shut your eyes, and you immediately devise a perfect millennium for mankind. When you went away this afternoon I set to work at once and have already invented three systems, now I am preparing the fourth. It is true that at first one must refute everything that has gone before, but from the crocodile it is so easy to refute it; besides, it all becomes clearer, seen from the inside of the crocodile... There are some drawbacks, though small ones, in my position, however; it is somewhat damp here and covered with a sort of slime; moreover, there is a smell of indiarubber like the smell of my old galoshes. That is all, there are no other drawbacks.'

'Ivan Matveitch,' I interrupted, 'all this is a miracle in which I can scarcely believe. And can you, can you intend never to dine again?'

'What trivial nonsense you are troubling about, you thoughtless, frivolous creature! I talk to you about great ideas, and you... Understand that I am sufficiently nourished by the great ideas which light up the darkness in which I am enveloped. The good-natured proprietor has, however, after consulting the kindly Mutter, decided with her that they will every morning insert into the monster's jaws a bent metal tube, something like a whistle pipe, by means of which I can absorb coffee or broth with bread soaked in it. The pipe has already been bespoken in the neighbourhood, but I think this is superfluous luxury. I hope to live at least a thousand years, if it is true that crocodiles live so long, which, by the way—good thing I thought of it—you had better look up in some natural history tomorrow and tell me, for I may have been mistaken and have mixed it up with some excavated monster. There is only one reflection rather troubles me: as I am dressed in cloth and have boots on, the crocodile can obviously not digest me. Besides, I am alive, and so am opposing the process of digestion with my whole willpower; for you can understand that I do not wish to be turned into what all nourishment turns into, for that would be too humiliating for me. But there is one thing I am afraid of: in a thousand years the cloth of my coat, unfortunately of Russian make, may decay, and then, left without clothing, I might perhaps, in spite of my indignation, begin to be digested; and though by day nothing would induce me to allow it, at night, in my sleep, when a man's will deserts him, I may be overtaken by the humiliating destiny of a potato, a pancake, or veal. Such an idea reduces me to fury. This alone is an argument for the revision of the tariff and the encouragement of the importation of English cloth, which is stronger and so will withstand Nature longer when one is swallowed by a crocodile. At the first opportunity I will impart this idea to some statesman and at the same time to the political writers on our Petersburg dailies. Let them publish it abroad. I trust this will not be the only idea they will borrow from me. I foresee that every morning a regular crowd of them, provided with quarter-roubles from the editorial office, will be flocking round me to seize my ideas on the telegrams of the previous day. In brief, the future presents itself to me in the rosiest light.'

'Fever, fever!' I whispered to myself.

'My friend, and freedom?' I asked, wishing to learn his views thoroughly. 'You are, so to speak, in prison, while every man has a right to the enjoyment of freedom.'

'You are a fool,' he answered. 'Savages love independence,

wise men love order; and if there is no order…'

'Ivan Matveitch, spare me, please!'

'Hold your tongue and listen!' he squealed, vexed at my interrupting him. 'Never has my spirit soared as now. In my narrow refuge there is only one thing that I dread—the literary criticisms of the monthlies and the hiss of our satirical papers. I am afraid that thoughtless visitors, stupid and envious people and nihilists in general, may turn me into ridicule. But I will take measures. I am impatiently awaiting the response of the public tomorrow, and especially the opinion of the newspapers. You must tell me about the papers tomorrow.'

'Very good; tomorrow I will bring a perfect pile of papers with me.'

'Tomorrow it is too soon to expect reports in the newspapers, for it will take four days for it to be advertised. But from today come to me every evening by the back way through the yard. I am intending to employ you as my secretary. You shall read the newspapers and magazines to me, and I will dictate to you my ideas and give you commissions. Be particularly careful not to forget the foreign telegrams. Let all the European telegrams be here every day. But enough; most likely you are sleepy by now. Go home, and do not think of what I said just now about criticisms: I am not afraid of it, for the critics themselves are in a critical position. One has only to be wise and virtuous and one will certainly get on to a pedestal. If not Socrates, then Diogenes, or perhaps both of them together—that is my future role among mankind.'

So frivolously and boastfully did Ivan Matveitch hasten to express himself before me, like feverish weak-willed women who, as we are told by the proverb, cannot keep a secret. All that he told me about the crocodile struck me as most suspicious. How was it possible that the crocodile was absolutely hollow? I don't mind betting that he was bragging from vanity and partly to humiliate me. It is true that he was an invalid and one must make allowances for invalids; but I must frankly confess, I never could endure Ivan Matveitch. I have been trying all my life, from a child up, to escape from his tutelage and have not been able to! A thousand times over I have been tempted to break with him altogether, and every time I have been drawn to him again, as though I were still hoping to prove something to him or to revenge myself on him. A strange thing, this friendship! I can positively assert that nine-tenths of my friendship for him was made up of malice. On this occasion, however, we parted with genuine feeling.

'Your friend a very clever man!' the German said to me in an undertone as he moved to see me out; he had been listening all the time attentively to our conversation.

'À propos,' I said, 'while I think of it: how much would you ask for your crocodile in case any one wanted to buy it?'

Ivan Matveitch, who heard the question, was waiting with curiosity for the answer; it was evident that he did not want the German to ask too little; anyway, he cleared his throat in a peculiar way on hearing my question.

At first the German would not listen—was positively angry.

'No one will dare my own crocodile to buy!' he cried furiously, and turned as red as a boiled lobster. 'Me not want to sell the crocodile! I would not for the crocodile a million thalers take. I took a hundred and thirty thalers from the public today, and I shall tomorrow ten thousand take, and then a hundred thousand every day I shall take. I will not him sell.'

Ivan Matveitch positively chuckled with satisfaction. Controlling myself—for I felt it was a duty to my friend—I hinted coolly and reasonably to the crazy German that his calculations were not quite correct, that if he makes a hundred thousand every day, all Petersburg will have visited him in four days, and then there will be no one left to bring him roubles, that life and death are in God's hands, that the crocodile may burst or Ivan Matveitch may fall ill and die, and so on and so on.

The German grew pensive.

'I will him drops from the chemist's get,' he said, after pondering, 'and will save your friend that he die not.'

'Drops are all very well,' I answered, 'but consider, too, that the thing may get into the law courts. Ivan Matveitch's wife may demand the restitution of her lawful spouse. You are intending to get rich, but do you intend to give Elena Ivanovna a pension?'

'No, me not intend,' said the German in stern decision.

'No, we not intend,' said the Mutter, with positive malignancy.

'And so would it not be better for you to accept something now, at once, a secure and solid though moderate sum, than to leave things to chance? I ought to tell you that I am inquiring simply from curiosity.'

The German drew the Mutter aside to consult with her in a corner where there stood a case with the largest and ugliest monkey of his collection.

'Well, you will see!' said Ivan Matveitch.

As for me, I was at that moment burning with the desire, first, to give the German a thrashing, next, to give the Mutter an even sounder one, and, thirdly, to give Ivan Matveitch the soundest thrashing of all for his boundless vanity. But all this paled beside the answer of the rapacious German.

After consultation with the Mutter he demanded for his crocodile fifty thousand roubles in bonds of the last Russian loan with lottery voucher attached, a brick house in Gorohovy Street with a chemist's shop attached, and in addition the rank of Russian colonel.

'You see!' Ivan Matveitch cried triumphantly. 'I told you so! Apart from this last senseless desire for the rank of a colonel, he is perfectly right, for he fully understands the present value of the monster he is exhibiting. The economic principle before everything!'

'Upon my word!' I cried furiously to the German. 'But what should you be made a colonel for? What exploit have you performed? What service have you done? In what way have you gained military glory? You are really crazy!'

'Crazy!' cried the German, offended. 'No, a person very sensible, but you very stupid! I have a colonel deserved for that I have a crocodile shown and in him a live hofrath sitting! And a Russian can a crocodile not show and a live hofrath in him sitting! Me extremely clever man and much wish colonel to be!'

'Well, good-bye, then, Ivan Matveitch!' I cried, shaking with fury, and I went out of the crocodile room almost at a run.

I felt that in another minute I could not have answered for myself. The unnatural expectations of these two blockheads were insupportable. The cold air refreshed me and somewhat moderated my indignation. At last, after spitting vigorously fifteen times on each side, I took a cab, got home, undressed and flung myself into bed. What vexed me more than anything was my having become his secretary. Now I was to die of boredom there every evening, doing the duty of a true friend! I was ready to beat myself for it, and I did, in fact, after putting out the candle and pulling up the bedclothes, punch myself several times on the head and various parts of my body. That somewhat relieved me, and at last I fell asleep fairly soundly, in fact, for I was very tired. All night long I could dream of nothing but monkeys, but towards morning I dreamt of Elena Ivanovna.

IV

The monkeys I dreamed about, I surmise, because they were shut up in the case at the German's; but Elena Ivanovna was a different story.

I may as well say at once, I loved the lady, but I make haste—post-haste—to make a qualification. I loved her as a father, neither more nor less. I judge that because I often felt an irresistible desire to kiss her little head or her rosy cheek. And though I never carried out this inclination, I would not have refused even to kiss her lips. And not merely her lips, but her teeth, which always gleamed so charmingly like two rows of pretty, well-matched pearls when she laughed. She laughed extraordinarily often. Ivan Matveitch in demonstrative moments used to call her his 'darling absurdity'—a name extremely happy and appropriate. She was a perfect sugar-plum, and that was all one could say of her. Therefore I am utterly at a loss to understand what possessed Ivan Matveitch to imagine his wife as a Russian Yevgenia Tour? Anyway, my dream, with the exception of the monkeys, left a most pleasant impression upon me, and going over all the incidents of the previous day as I drank my morning cup of tea, I resolved to go and see Elena Ivanovna at once on my way to the office—which, indeed, I was bound to do as the friend of the family.

In a tiny little room out of the bedroom—the so-called little drawing-room, though their big drawing-room was little too—Elena Ivanovna was sitting, in some half-transparent morning wrapper, on a smart little sofa before a little tea-table, drinking coffee out of a little cup in which she was dipping a minute biscuit. She was ravishingly pretty, but struck me as being at the same time rather pensive.

'Ah, that's you, naughty man!' she said, greeting me with an absent-minded smile. 'Sit down, feather-head, have some coffee. Well, what were you doing yesterday? Were you at the masquerade?'

'Why, were you? I don't go, you know. Besides, yesterday I was visiting our captive...' I sighed and assumed a pious expression as I took the coffee.

'Whom?... What captive?... Oh, yes! Poor fellow! Well, how is he—bored? Do you know...I wanted to ask you... I suppose I can ask for a divorce now?'

'A divorce!' I cried in indignation and almost spilled the coffee. 'It's that swarthy fellow,' I thought to myself bitterly.

There was a certain swarthy gentleman with little moustaches who was something in the architectural line, and who came far too often to see them, and was extremely skilful in amusing Elena Ivanovna. I must confess I hated him and there was no doubt that he had succeeded in seeing Elena Ivanovna yesterday either at the masquerade or even here, and putting all sorts of nonsense into her head.

'Why,' Elena Ivanovna rattled off hurriedly, as though it were a lesson she had learnt, 'if he is going to stay on in the crocodile, perhaps not come back all his life, while I sit waiting for him here! A husband ought to live at home, and not in a crocodile...'

'But this was an unforeseen occurrence,' I was beginning, in very comprehensible agitation.

'Oh, no, don't talk to me, I won't listen, I won't listen,' she cried, suddenly getting quite cross. 'You are always against me, you wretch! There's no doing anything with you, you will never give me any advice! Other people tell me that I can get a divorce because Ivan Matveitch will not get his salary now.'

'Elena Ivanovna! is it you I hear!' I exclaimed pathetically. 'What villain could have put such an idea into your head? And divorce on such a trivial ground as a salary is quite impossible. And poor Ivan Matveitch, poor Ivan Matveitch is, so to speak, burning with love for you even in the bowels of the monster. What's more, he is melting away with love like a lump of sugar. Yesterday while you were enjoying yourself at the masquerade, he was saying that he might in the last resort send for you as his lawful spouse to join him in the entrails of the monster, especially as it appears the crocodile is exceedingly roomy, not only able to accommodate two but even three persons...'

And then I told her all that interesting part of my conversation the night before with Ivan Matveitch.

'What, what!' she cried, in surprise. 'You want me to get into the monster too, to be with Ivan Matveitch? What an idea! And how am I to get in there, in my hat and crinoline? Heavens, what foolishness! And what should I look like while I was getting into it, and very likely there would be some one there to see me! It's absurd! And what should I have to eat there? And...and...and what should I do there when... Oh, my goodness, what will they think of next?... And what should I have to amuse me there?... You say there's a smell of gutta-percha? And what should I do if we quarrelled—should we have to go on staying there side by side? Foo, how horrid!'

'I agree, I agree with all those arguments, my sweet Elena Ivanovna,' I interrupted, striving to express myself with that natural enthusiasm which always overtakes a man when he feels the truth is on his side. 'But one thing you have not appreciated in all this, you have not realized that he cannot live without you if he is inviting you there; that is a proof of love, passionate, faithful, ardent love... You have thought too little of his love, dear Elena Ivanovna!'

'I won't, I won't, I won't hear anything about it!' waving me off with her pretty little hand with glistening pink nails that had just been washed and polished. 'Horrid man! You will reduce me to tears! Get into it yourself, if you like the prospect. You are his friend, get in and keep him company, and spend your life discussing some tedious science...'

'You are wrong to laugh at this suggestion'—I checked the frivolous woman with dignity—'Ivan Matveitch has invited me as it is. You, of course, are summoned there by duty; for me, it would be an act of generosity. But when Ivan Matveitch described to me last night the elasticity of the crocodile, he hinted very plainly that there would be room not only for you two, but for me also as a friend of the family, especially if I wished to join you, and therefore...'

'How so, the three of us?' cried Elena Ivanovna, looking at me in surprise. 'Why, how should we...are we going to be all three there together? Ha-ha-ha! How silly you both are! Ha-ha-ha! I shall certainly pinch you all the time, you wretch! Ha-ha-ha! Ha-ha-ha!'

And falling back on the sofa, she laughed till she cried. All this—the tears and the laughter—were so fascinating that I could not resist rushing eagerly to kiss her hand, which she did not oppose, though she did pinch my ears lightly as a sign of reconciliation.

Then we both grew very cheerful, and I described to her in detail all Ivan Matveitch's plans. The thought of her evening receptions and her salon pleased her very much.

'Only I should need a great many new dresses,' she observed, 'and so Ivan Matveitch must send me as much of his salary as possible and as soon as possible. Only...only I don't know about that,' she added thoughtfully. 'How can he be brought here in the tank? That's very absurd. I don't want my husband to be carried about in a tank. I should feel quite ashamed for my visitors to see it... I don't want that, no, I don't.'

'By the way, while I think of it, was Timofey Semyonitch here yesterday?'

'Oh, yes, he was; he came to comfort me, and do you know, we played cards all the time. He played for sweetmeats, and if I lost he was to kiss my hands. What a wretch he is! And only fancy, he almost came to the masquerade with me, really!'

'He was carried away by his feelings!' I observed. 'And who would not be with you, you charmer?'

'Oh, get along with your compliments! Stay, I'll give you

a pinch as a parting present. I've learnt to pinch awfully well lately. Well, what do you say to that? By the way, you say Ivan Matveitch spoke several times of me yesterday?'

'N-no, not exactly... I must say he is thinking more now of the fate of humanity, and wants...'

'Oh, let him! You needn't go on! I am sure it's fearfully boring. I'll go and see him some time. I shall certainly go tomorrow. Only not today; I've got a headache, and besides, there will be such a lot of people there today... They'll say, "That's his wife," and I shall feel ashamed... Good-bye. You will be...there this evening, won't you?'

'To see him, yes. He asked me to go and take him the papers.'

'That's capital. Go and read to him. But don't come and see me today. I am not well, and perhaps I may go and see some one. Good-bye, you naughty man.'

'It's that swarthy fellow is going to see her this evening,' I thought.

At the office, of course, I gave no sign of being consumed by these cares and anxieties. But soon I noticed some of the most progressive papers seemed to be passing particularly rapidly from hand to hand among my colleagues, and were being read with an extremely serious expression of face. The first one that reached me was the *News-sheet*, a paper of no particular party but humanitarian in general, for which it was regarded with contempt among us, though it was read. Not without surprise I read in it the following paragraph:

'Yesterday strange rumours were circulating among the spacious ways and sumptuous buildings of our vast metropolis. A certain well-known bon-vivant of the highest society, probably weary of the cuisine at Borel's and at the X Club, went into the Arcade, into the place where an immense crocodile recently brought to the metropolis is being exhibited, and insisted on its being prepared for his dinner. After bargaining with the proprietor he at once set to work to devour him (that is, not the proprietor, a very meek and punctilious German, but his crocodile), cutting juicy morsels with his penknife from the living animal, and swallowing them with extraordinary rapidity. By degrees the whole crocodile disappeared into the vast recesses of his stomach, so that he was even on the point of attacking an ichneumon, a constant companion of the crocodile, probably imagining that the latter would be as savoury. We are by no means opposed to that new article of diet with which foreign gourmands have long been familiar. We have, indeed, predicted that it would come. English lords and travellers make up regular parties for catching crocodiles in Egypt, and consume the back of the monster cooked like beefsteak, with mustard, onions and potatoes. The French who followed in the train of Lesseps prefer the paws baked in hot ashes, which they do, however, in opposition to the English, who laugh at them. Probably both ways would be appreciated among us. For our part, we are delighted at a new branch of industry, of which our great and varied fatherland stands pre-eminently in need. Probably before a year is out crocodiles will be brought in hundreds to replace this first one, lost in the stomach of a Petersburg gourmand. And why should not the crocodile be acclimatized among us in Russia? If the water of the Neva is too cold for these interesting strangers, there are ponds in the capital and rivers and lakes outside it. Why not breed crocodiles at Pargolovo, for instance, or at Pavlovsk, in the Presnensky Ponds and in Samoteka in Moscow? While providing agreeable, wholesome nourishment for our fastidious gourmands, they might at the same time entertain the ladies who walk about these ponds and instruct the children in natural history. The crocodile skin might be used for making jewel-cases, boxes, cigar-cases, pocketbooks, and possibly more than one thousand saved up in the greasy notes that are peculiarly beloved of merchants might be laid by in crocodile skin. We hope to return more than once to this interesting topic.'

Though I had foreseen something of the sort, yet the reckless inaccuracy of the paragraph overwhelmed me. Finding no one with whom to share my impression, I turned to Prohor Savvitch who was sitting opposite to me, and noticed that the latter had been watching me for some time, while in his hand he held the *Voice* as though he were on the point of passing it to me. Without a word he took the *News-sheet* from me, and as he handed me the *Voice* he drew a line with his nail against an article to which he probably wished to call my attention. This Prohor Savvitch was a very queer man: a taciturn old bachelor, he was not on intimate terms with any of us, scarcely spoke to any one in the office, always had an opinion of his own about everything, but could not bear to impart it to any one. He lived alone. Hardly any one among us had ever been in his lodging.

This was what I read in the *Voice*.

'Every one knows that we are progressive and humanitarian and want to be on a level with Europe in this respect. But in spite of all our exertions and the efforts of our paper we are still far from maturity, as may be judged from the shocking incident which took place yesterday in the Arcade and which we predicted long ago. A foreigner arrives in the capital bringing with him a crocodile which he begins exhibiting in the Arcade. We immediately hasten to welcome a new branch of useful industry such as our powerful and varied fatherland stands in great need of. Suddenly yesterday at four o'clock in the afternoon a gentleman of exceptional stoutness enters the foreigner's shop in an intoxicated condition, pays his entrance money, and immediately without any warning leaps into the jaws of the crocodile, who was forced, of course, to swallow him, if only from an instinct of self-preservation, to avoid being crushed. Tumbling into the inside of the crocodile, the stranger at once dropped asleep. Neither the shouts of the foreign proprietor, nor the lamentations of his terrified family, nor threats to send for the police made the slightest impression. Within the crocodile was heard nothing but laughter and a promise to flay him (sic), though the poor mammal, compelled to swallow such a mass, was vainly shedding tears. An uninvited guest is worse than a Tartar. But in spite of the proverb the insolent visitor would not leave. We do not know how to explain such barbarous incidents which prove our lack of culture and disgrace us in the eyes of foreigners. The recklessness of the Russian temperament has found a fresh outlet. It may be asked what was the object of the uninvited visitor? A warm and comfortable abode? But there are many excellent houses in the capital with very cheap and comfortable lodgings, with the Neva water laid on, and a staircase lighted by gas, frequently with a hall-porter maintained by the proprietor. We would call our readers' attention to the barbarous treatment of domestic animals: it is difficult, of course, for the crocodile to digest such a mass all at once, and now he lies swollen out to the size of a mountain, awaiting death in insufferable agonies. In Europe persons guilty of inhumanity towards domestic animals have long been punished by law. But in spite of our European enlightenment, in spite of our European pavements, in spite of the European architecture of our houses, we are still far from shaking off our time-honoured traditions.

"Though the houses are new, the conventions are old."

'And, indeed, the houses are not new, at least the staircases in them are not. We have more than once in our paper alluded to the fact that in the Petersburg Side in the house of the merchant Lukyanov the steps of the wooden staircase have decayed, fallen away, and have long been a danger for Afimya Skapidarov, a soldier's wife who works in the house, and is often obliged to go up the stairs with water or armfuls of wood. At last our predictions have come true: yesterday evening at half past eight Afimya Skapidarov fell down with a basin of soup and broke her leg. We do not know whether Lukyanov will mend his staircase now, Russians are often wise after the event, but the victim of Russian carelessness has by now been taken to the hospital. In the same way we shall never cease to maintain that the house-porters who clear away the mud from the wooden pavement in the Viborgsky Side ought not to spatter the legs of passers-by, but should throw the mud up into heaps as is done in Europe,' and so on, and so on.

'What's this?' I asked in some perplexity, looking at Prohor Savvitch. 'What's the meaning of it?'

'How do you mean?'

'Why, upon my word! Instead of pitying Ivan Matveitch, they pity the crocodile!'

'What of it? They have pity even for a beast, a mammal. We must be up to Europe, mustn't we? They have a very warm feeling for crocodiles there too. He-he-he!'

Saying this, queer old Prohor Savvitch dived into his papers and would not utter another word.

I stuffed the *Voice* and the *News-sheet* into my pocket and collected as many old copies of the newspapers as I could find for Ivan Matveitch's diversion in the evening, and though the evening was far off, yet on this occasion I slipped away from the office early to go to the Arcade and look, if only from a distance, at what was going on there, and to listen to the various remarks and currents of opinion. I foresaw that there would be a regular crush there, and turned up the collar of my coat to meet it. I somehow felt rather shy—so unaccustomed are we to publicity. But I feel that I have no right to report my own prosaic feelings when faced with this remarkable and original incident.

5

BOBOK:

FROM SOMEBODY'S DIARY

Semyon Ardalyonovitch said to me all of a sudden the day before yesterday: 'Why, will you ever be sober, Ivan Ivanovitch? Tell me that, pray.'

A strange requirement. I did not resent it, I am a timid man; but here they have actually made me out mad. An artist painted my portrait as it happened: 'After all, you are a literary man,' he said. I submitted, he exhibited it. I read: 'Go and look at that morbid face suggesting insanity.'

It may be so, but think of putting it so bluntly into print. In print everything ought to be decorous; there ought to be ideals, while instead of that...

Say it indirectly, at least; that's what you have style for. But no, he doesn't care to do it indirectly. Nowadays humour and a fine style have disappeared, and abuse is accepted as wit. I do not resent it: but God knows I am not enough of a literary man to go out of my mind. I have written a novel, it has not been published. I have written articles—they have been refused. Those articles I took about from one editor to another; everywhere they refused them: you have no salt, they told me. 'What sort of salt do you want?' I asked with a jeer. 'Attic salt?'

They did not even understand. For the most part I translate from the French for the booksellers. I write advertisements for shopkeepers too: 'Unique opportunity! Fine tea, from our own plantations...' I made a nice little sum over a panegyric on his deceased excellency Pyotr Matveyitch. I compiled the 'Art of pleasing the ladies,' a commission from a bookseller. I have brought out some six little works of this kind in the course of my life. I am thinking of making a collection of the bon mots of Voltaire, but am afraid it may seem a little flat to our people. Voltaire's no good now; nowadays we want a cudgel, not Voltaire. We knock each other's last teeth out nowadays. Well, so that's the whole extent of my literary activity. Though indeed I do send round letters to the editors gratis and fully signed. I give them all sorts of counsels and admonitions, criticize and point out the true path. The letter I sent last week to an editor's office was the fortieth I had sent in the last two years. I have wasted four roubles over stamps alone for them. My temper is at the bottom of it all.

I believe that the artist who painted me did so not for the sake of literature, but for the sake of two symmetrical warts on my forehead, a natural phenomenon, he would say. They have no ideas, so now they are out for phenomena. And didn't he succeed in getting my warts in his portrait—to the life. That is what they call realism.

And as to madness, a great many people were put down as mad among us last year. And in such language! 'With such original talent'...'and yet, after all, it appears'...'however, one ought to have foreseen it long ago.' That is rather artful; so that from the point of view of pure art one may really commend it. Well, but after all, these so-called madmen have turned out cleverer than ever. So it seems the critics can call them mad, but they cannot produce any one better.

The wisest of all, in my opinion, is he who can, if only once a month, call himself a fool—a faculty unheard of nowadays. In old days, once a year at any rate a fool would recognize that he was a fool, but nowadays not a bit of it. And they have so muddled things up that there is no telling a fool from a wise man. They have done that on purpose.

I remember a witty Spaniard saying when, two hundred and fifty years ago, the French built their first madhouses: 'They have shut up all their fools in a house apart, to make sure that they are wise men themselves.' Just so: you don't show your own wisdom by shutting some one else in a madhouse. 'K has gone out of his mind, means that we are sane now.' No, it doesn't mean that yet.

Hang it though, why am I maundering on? I go on grumbling and grumbling. Even my maidservant is sick of me. Yesterday a friend came to see me. 'Your style is changing,' he said; 'it is choppy: you chop and chop—and then a parenthesis, then a parenthesis in the parenthesis, then you stick in something else in brackets, then you begin chopping and chopping again.'

The friend is right. Something strange is happening to me. My character is changing and my head aches. I am beginning to see and hear strange things, not voices exactly, but as though some one beside me were muttering, 'bobok, bobok, bobok!'

What's the meaning of this bobok? I must divert my mind.

I went out in search of diversion, I hit upon a funeral. A distant relation—a collegiate counsellor, however. A widow and five daughters, all marriageable young ladies. What must it come to even to keep them in slippers. Their father managed it, but now there is only a little pension. They will have to eat humble pie. They have always received me ungraciously. And indeed I should not have gone to the funeral now had it not been for a peculiar circumstance. I followed the procession to the cemetery with the rest; they were stuck-up and held aloof from me. My uniform was certainly rather shabby. It's five-and-twenty years, I believe, since I was at the cemetery; what a wretched place!

To begin with the smell. There were fifteen hearses, with palls varying in expensiveness; there were actually two catafalques. One was a general's and one some lady's. There were many mourners, a great deal of feigned mourning and a great deal of open gaiety. The clergy have nothing to complain of; it brings them a good income. But the smell, the smell. I should not like to be one of the clergy here.

I kept glancing at the faces of the dead cautiously, distrusting my impressionability. Some had a mild expression, some looked unpleasant. As a rule the smiles were disagreeable, and in some cases very much so. I don't like them; they haunt one's dreams.

During the service I went out of the church into the air: it was a grey day, but dry. It was cold too, but then it was October. I walked about among the tombs. They are of different grades. The third grade cost thirty roubles; it's decent and not so very dear. The first two grades are tombs in the church and under the porch; they cost a pretty penny. On this occasion they were burying in tombs of the third grade six persons, among them the general and the lady.

I looked into the graves—and it was horrible: water and such water! Absolutely green, and…but there, why talk of it! The gravedigger was baling it out every minute. I went out while the service was going on and strolled outside the gates. Close by was an almshouse, and a little further off there was a restaurant. It was not a bad little restaurant: there was lunch and everything. There were lots of the mourners here. I noticed a great deal of gaiety and genuine heartiness. I had something to eat and drink.

Then I took part in the bearing of the coffin from the church to the grave. Why is it that corpses in their coffins are so heavy? They say it is due to some sort of inertia, that the body is no longer directed by its owner...or some nonsense of that sort, in opposition to the laws of mechanics and common sense. I don't like to hear people who have nothing but a general education venture to solve the problems that require special knowledge; and with us that's done continually. Civilians love to pass opinions about subjects that are the province of the soldier and even of the field-marshal; while men who have been educated as engineers prefer discussing philosophy and political economy.

I did not go to the requiem service. I have some pride, and if I am only received owing to some special necessity, why force myself on their dinners, even if it be a funeral dinner. The only thing I don't understand is why I stayed at the cemetery; I sat on a tombstone and sank into appropriate reflections.

I began with the Moscow exhibition and ended with reflecting upon astonishment in the abstract. My deductions about astonishment were these:

'To be surprised at everything is stupid of course, and to be astonished at nothing is a great deal more becoming and for some reason accepted as good form. But that is not really true. To my mind to be astonished at nothing is much more stupid than to be astonished at everything. And, moreover, to be astonished at nothing is almost the same as feeling respect for nothing. And indeed a stupid man is incapable of feeling respect.'

'But what I desire most of all is to feel respect. I *thirst* to feel respect,' one of my acquaintances said to me the other day.

He thirsts to feel respect! Goodness, I thought, what would happen to you if you dared to print that nowadays?

At that point I sank into forgetfulness. I don't like reading the epitaphs of tombstones: they are everlastingly the same. An unfinished sandwich was lying on the tombstone near me; stupid and inappropriate. I threw it on the ground, as it was not bread but only a sandwich. Though I believe it is not a sin to throw bread on the earth, but only on the floor. I must look it up in Suvorin's calendar.

I suppose I sat there a long time—too long a time, in fact; I must have lain down on a long stone which was of the shape of a marble coffin. And how it happened I don't know, but I began to hear things of all sorts being said. At first I did not pay attention to it, but treated it with contempt. But the conversation went on. I heard muffled sounds as though the speakers' mouths were covered with a pillow, and at the same time they were distinct and very near. I came to myself, sat up and began listening attentively.

'Your Excellency, it's utterly impossible. You led hearts, I return your lead, and here you play the seven of diamonds. You ought to have given me a hint about diamonds.'

'What, play by hard and fast rules? Where is the charm of that?'

'You must, your Excellency. One can't do anything without something to go upon. We must play with dummy, let one hand not be turned up.'

'Well, you won't find a dummy here.'

What conceited words! And it was queer and unexpected. One was such a ponderous, dignified voice, the other softly suave; I should not have believed it if I had not heard it myself. I had not been to the requiem dinner, I believe. And yet how could they be playing preference here and what general was this? That the sounds came from under the tombstones of that there could be no doubt. I bent down and read on the tomb:

'Here lies the body of Major-General Pervoyedov…a cavalier of such and such orders.' Hm! 'Passed away in August of this year…fifty-seven… Rest, beloved ashes, till the joyful dawn!'

Hm, dash it, it really is a general! There was no monument

on the grave from which the obsequious voice came, there was only a tombstone. He must have been a fresh arrival. From his voice he was a lower court councillor.

'Oh-ho-ho-ho!' I heard in a new voice a dozen yards from the general's resting-place, coming from quite a fresh grave. The voice belonged to a man and a plebeian, mawkish with its affectation of religious fervour. 'Oh-ho-ho-ho!'

'Oh, here he is hiccupping again!' cried the haughty and disdainful voice of an irritated lady, apparently of the highest society. 'It is an affliction to be by this shopkeeper!'

'I didn't hiccup; why, I've had nothing to eat. It's simply my nature. Really, madam, you don't seem able to get rid of your caprices here.'

'Then why did you come and lie down here?'

'They put me here, my wife and little children put me here, I did not lie down here of myself. The mystery of death! And I would not have lain down beside you not for any money; I lie here as befitting my fortune, judging by the price. For we can always do that—pay for a tomb of the third grade.'

'You made money, I suppose? You fleeced people?'

'Fleece you, indeed! We haven't seen the colour of your money since January. There's a little bill against you at the shop.'

'Well, that's really stupid; to try and recover debts here is too stupid, to my thinking! Go to the surface. Ask my niece—she is my heiress.'

'There's no asking any one now, and no going anywhere. We have both reached our limit and, before the judgment-seat of God, are equal in our sins.'

'In our sins,' the lady mimicked him contemptuously. 'Don't dare to speak to me.'

'Oh-ho-ho-ho!'

'You see, the shopkeeper obeys the lady, your Excellency.'

'Why shouldn't he?'

'Why, your Excellency, because, as we all know, things are different here.'

'Different? How?'

'We are dead, so to speak, your Excellency.'

'Oh, yes! But still...'

Well, this is an entertainment, it is a fine show, I must say! If it has come to this down here, what can one expect on the surface? But what a queer business! I went on listening, however, though with extreme indignation.

'Yes, I should like a taste of life! Yes, you know...I should like a taste of life.' I heard a new voice suddenly somewhere in the space between the general and the irritable lady.

'Do you hear, your Excellency, our friend is at the same game again. For three days at a time he says nothing, and then he bursts out with "I should like a taste of life, yes, a taste of life!" And with such appetite, he-he!'

'And such frivolity.'

'It gets hold of him, your Excellency, and do you know, he is growing sleepy, quite sleepy—he has been here since April; and then all of a sudden "I should like a taste of life!"'

'It is rather dull, though,' observed his Excellency.

'It is, your Excellency. Shall we tease Avdotya Ignatyevna again, he-he?'

'No, spare me, please. I can't endure that quarrelsome virago.'

'And I can't endure either of you,' cried the virago disdainfully. 'You are both of you bores and can't tell me anything ideal. I know one little story about you, your Excellency—don't turn up your nose, please—how a manservant swept you out from under a married couple's bed one morning.'

'Nasty woman,' the general muttered through his teeth.

'Avdotya Ignatyevna, ma'am,' the shopkeeper wailed

suddenly again, 'my dear lady, don't be angry, but tell me, am I going through the ordeal by torment now, or is it something else?'

'Ah, he is at it again, as I expected! For there's a smell from him which means he is turning round!'

'I am not turning round, ma'am, and there's no particular smell from me, for I've kept my body whole as it should be, while you're regularly high. For the smell is really horrible even for a place like this. I don't speak of it, merely from politeness.'

'Ah, you horrid, insulting wretch! He positively stinks and talks about me.'

'Oh-ho-ho-ho! If only the time for my requiem would come quickly: I should hear their tearful voices over my head, my wife's lament and my children's soft weeping!…'

'Well, that's a thing to fret for! They'll stuff themselves with funeral rice and go home… Oh, I wish somebody would wake up!'

'Avdotya Ignatyevna,' said the insinuating government clerk, 'wait a bit, the new arrivals will speak.'

'And are there any young people among them?'

'Yes, there are, Avdotya Ignatyevna. There are some not more than lads.'

'Oh, how welcome that would be!'

'Haven't they begun yet?' inquired his Excellency.

'Even those who came the day before yesterday haven't awakened yet, your Excellency. As you know, they sometimes don't speak for a week. It's a good job that today and yesterday and the day before they brought a whole lot. As it is, they are all last year's for seventy feet round.'

'Yes, it will be interesting.'

'Yes, your Excellency, they buried Tarasevitch, the privy councillor, today. I knew it from the voices. I know his nephew, he helped to lower the coffin just now.'

'Hm, where is he, then?'

'Five steps from you, your Excellency, on the left... Almost at your feet. You should make his acquaintance, your Excellency.'

'Hm, no—it's not for me to make advances.'

'Oh, he will begin of himself, your Excellency. He will be flattered. Leave it to me, your Excellency, and I...'

'Oh, oh!...What is happening to me?' croaked the frightened voice of a new arrival.

'A new arrival, your Excellency, a new arrival, thank God! And how quick he's been! Sometimes they don't say a word for a week.'

'Oh, I believe it's a young man!' Avdotya Ignatyevna cried shrilly.

'I...I...it was a complication, and so sudden!' faltered the young man again. 'Only the evening before, Schultz said to me, "There's a complication," and I died suddenly before morning. Oh! Oh!'

'Well, there's no help for it, young man,' the general observed graciously, evidently pleased at a new arrival. 'You must be comforted. You are kindly welcome to our Vale of Jehoshaphat, so to call it. We are kind-hearted people, you will come to know us and appreciate us. Major-General Vassili Vassilitch Pervoyedov, at your service.'

'Oh, no, no! Certainly not! I was at Schultz's; I had a complication, you know, at first it was my chest and a cough, and then I caught a cold: my lungs and influenza...and all of a sudden, quite unexpectedly...the worst of all was its being so unexpected.'

'You say it began with the chest,' the government clerk put in suavely, as though he wished to reassure the new arrival.

'Yes, my chest and catarrh and then no catarrh, but still the chest, and I couldn't breathe...and you know...'

'I know, I know. But if it was the chest you ought to have

gone to Ecke and not to Schultz.'

'You know, I kept meaning to go to Botkin's, and all at once...'

'Botkin is quite prohibitive,' observed the general.

'Oh, no, he is not forbidding at all; I've heard he is so attentive and foretells everything beforehand.'

'His Excellency was referring to his fees,' the government clerk corrected him.

'Oh, not at all, he only asks three roubles, and he makes such an examination, and gives you a prescription...and I was very anxious to see him, for I have been told... Well, gentlemen, had I better go to Ecke or to Botkin?'

'What? To whom?' The general's corpse shook with agreeable laughter. The government clerk echoed it in falsetto.

'Dear boy, dear, delightful boy, how I love you!' Avdotya Ignatyevna squealed ecstatically. 'I wish they had put some one like you next to me.'

No, that was too much! And these were the dead of our times! Still, I ought to listen to more and not be in too great a hurry to draw conclusions. That snivelling new arrival—I remember him just now in his coffin—had the expression of a frightened chicken, the most revolting expression in the world! However, let us wait and see.

But what happened next was such a Bedlam that I could not keep it all in my memory. For a great many woke up at once; an official—a civil councillor—woke up, and began discussing at once the project of a new sub-committee in a government department and of the probable transfer of various functionaries in connection with the sub-committee—which very greatly interested the general. I must confess I learnt a great deal that was new myself, so much so that I marvelled at the channels by which one may sometimes in the metropolis learn government news. Then an engineer half woke up, but for a long time muttered absolute nonsense, so that our friends left off worrying him and let him lie till he was ready. At last the distinguished lady who had been buried in the morning under the catafalque showed symptoms of the reanimation of the tomb. Lebeziatnikov (for the obsequious lower court councillor whom I detested and who lay beside General Pervoyedov was called, it appears, Lebeziatnikov) became much excited, and surprised that they were all waking up so soon this time. I must own I was surprised too; though some of those who woke had been buried for three days, as, for instance, a very young girl of sixteen who kept giggling…giggling in a horrible and predatory way.

'Your Excellency, privy councillor Tarasevitch is waking!' Lebeziatnikov announced with extreme fussiness.

'Eh? What?' the privy councillor, waking up suddenly, mumbled, with a lisp of disgust. There was a note of ill-humoured peremptoriness in the sound of his voice.

I listened with curiosity—for during the last few days I had heard something about Tarasevitch—shocking and upsetting in the extreme.

'It's I, your Excellency, so far only I.'

'What is your petition? What do you want?'

'Merely to inquire after your Excellency's health; in these unaccustomed surroundings every one feels at first, as it were, oppressed… General Pervoyedov wishes to have the honour of making your Excellency's acquaintance, and hopes…'

'I've never heard of him.'

'Surely, your Excellency! General Pervoyedov, Vassili Vassilitch…'

'Are you General Pervoyedov?'

'No, your Excellency, I am only the lower court councillor Lebeziatnikov, at your service, but General Pervoyedov…'

'Nonsense! And I beg you to leave me alone.'

'Let him be.' General Pervoyedov at last himself checked with dignity the disgusting officiousness of his sycophant in the grave.

'He is not fully awake, your Excellency, you must consider that; it's the novelty of it all. When he is fully awake he will take it differently.'

'Let him be,' repeated the general.

'Vassili Vassilitch! Hey, your Excellency!' a perfectly new voice shouted loudly and aggressively from close beside Avdotya Ignatyevna. It was a voice of gentlemanly insolence, with the languid pronunciation now fashionable and an arrogant drawl. 'I've been watching you all for the last two hours. Do you remember me, Vassili Vassilitch? My name is Klinevitch, we met at the Volokonskys' where you, too, were received as a guest, I am sure I don't know why.'

'What, Count Pyotr Petrovitch?... Can it be really you... and at such an early age? How sorry I am to hear it.'

'Oh, I am sorry myself, though I really don't mind, and I want to amuse myself as far as I can everywhere. And I am not a count but a baron, only a baron. We are only a set of scurvy barons, risen from being flunkeys, but why I don't know and I don't care. I am only a scoundrel of the pseudo-aristocratic society, and I am regarded as "a charming polis-son". My father is a wretched little general, and my mother was at one time received en haut lieu. With the help of the Jew Zifel I forged fifty thousand rouble notes last year and then I informed against him, while Julie Charpentier de Lusignan carried off the money to Bordeaux. And only fancy, I was engaged to be married—to a girl still at school, three months under sixteen, with a dowry of ninety thousand. Avdotya Ignatyevna, do you remember how you seduced me fifteen years ago when I was a boy of fourteen in the Corps des Pages?'

'Ah, that's you, you rascal! Well, you are a godsend, anyway, for here...'

'You were mistaken in suspecting your neighbour, the business gentleman, of unpleasant fragrance... I said nothing, but I laughed. The stench came from me: they had to bury me in a nailed-up coffin.'

'Ugh, you horrid creature! Still, I am glad you are here; you can't imagine the lack of life and wit here.'

'Quite so, quite so, and I intend to start here something original. Your Excellency—I don't mean you, Pervoyedov— your Excellency the other one, Tarasevitch, the privy councillor! Answer! I am Klinevitch, who took you to Mlle Furie in Lent, do you hear?'

'I do, Klinevitch, and I am delighted, and trust me...'

'I wouldn't trust you with a halfpenny, and I don't care. I simply want to kiss you, dear old man, but luckily I can't. Do you know, gentlemen, what this grand-père's little game was? He died three or four days ago, and would you believe it, he left a deficit of four hundred thousand government money from the fund for widows and orphans. He was the sole person in control of it for some reason, so that his accounts were not audited for the last eight years. I can fancy what long faces they all have now, and what they call him. It's a delectable thought, isn't it? I have been wondering for the last year how a wretched old man of seventy, gouty and rheumatic, succeeded in preserving the physical energy for his debaucheries—and now the riddle is solved! Those widows and orphans—the very thought of them must have egged him on! I knew about it long ago, I was the only one who did know; it was Julie told me, and as soon as I discovered it, I attacked him in a friendly way at once in Easter week: 'Give me twenty-five thousand, if you don't they'll look into your accounts tomorrow.' And just fancy, he had only thirteen thousand left then, so it seems it was very apropos his dying now. Grand-père, grand-père, do you hear?'

'Cher Klinevitch, I quite agree with you, and there was no need for you...to go into such details. Life is so full of suffering and torment and so little to make up for it...that I wanted at last to be at rest, and so far as I can see I hope to get all I can from here too.'

'I bet that he has already sniffed Katiche Berestov!'

'Who? What Katiche?' There was a rapacious quiver in the old man's voice.

'A-ah, what Katiche? Why, here on the left, five paces from me and ten from you. She has been here for five days, and if only you knew, grand-père, what a little wretch she is! Of good family and breeding and a monster, a regular monster! I did not introduce her to any one there, I was the only one who knew her... Katiche, answer!'

'He-he-he!' the girl responded with a jangling laugh, in which there was a note of something as sharp as the prick of a needle. 'He-he-he!'

'And a little blonde?' the grand-père faltered, drawling out the syllables.

'He-he-he!'

'I...have long...I have long,' the old man faltered breathlessly, 'cherished the dream of a little fair thing of fifteen and just in such surroundings.'

'Ach, the monster!' cried Avdotya Ignatyevna.

'Enough!' Klinevitch decided. 'I see there is excellent material. We shall soon arrange things better. The great thing is to spend the rest of our time cheerfully; but what time? Hey, you, government clerk, Lebeziatnikov or whatever it is, I hear that's your name!'

'Semyon Yevseitch Lebeziatnikov, lower court councillor, at your service, very, very, very much delighted to meet you.'

'I don't care whether you are delighted or not, but you seem to know everything here. Tell me first of all how it is we can talk? I've been wondering ever since yesterday. We are dead and yet we are talking and seem to be moving—and yet we are not talking and not moving. What jugglery is this?'

'If you want an explanation, baron, Platon Nikolaevitch could give you one better than I.'

'What Platon Nikolaevitch is that? To the point. Don't beat about the bush.'

'Platon Nikolaevitch is our home-grown philosopher, scientist and Master of Arts. He has brought out several philosophical works, but for the last three months he has been getting quite drowsy, and there is no stirring him up now. Once a week he mutters something utterly irrelevant.'

'To the point, to the point!'

'He explains all this by the simplest fact, namely, that when we were living on the surface we mistakenly thought that death there was death. The body revives, as it were, here, the remains of life are concentrated, but only in consciousness. I don't know how to express it, but life goes on, as it were, by inertia. In his opinion everything is concentrated somewhere in consciousness and goes on for two or three months...sometimes even for half a year... There is one here, for instance, who is almost completely decomposed, but once every six weeks he suddenly utters one word, quite senseless of course, about some bobok,[1] "Bobok, bobok," but you see that an imperceptible speck of life is still warm within him.'

'It's rather stupid. Well, and how is it I have no sense of smell and yet I feel there's a stench?'

'That...he-he... Well, on that point our philosopher is a bit foggy. It's apropos of smell, he said, that the stench one

---

[1] i.e. small bean.

perceives here is, so to speak, moral—he-he! It's the stench of the soul, he says, that in these two or three months it may have time to recover itself...and this is, so to speak, the last mercy... Only, I think, baron, that these are mystic ravings very excusable in his position...'

'Enough; all the rest of it, I am sure, is nonsense. The great thing is that we have two or three months more of life and then—bobok! I propose to spend these two months as agreeably as possible, and so to arrange everything on a new basis. Gentlemen! I propose to cast aside all shame.'

'Ah, let us cast aside all shame, let us!' many voices could be heard saying; and strange to say, several new voices were audible, which must have belonged to others newly awakened. The engineer, now fully awake, boomed out his agreement with peculiar delight. The girl Katiche giggled gleefully.

'Oh, how I long to cast off all shame!' Avdotya Ignatyevna exclaimed rapturously.

'I say, if Avdotya Ignatyevna wants to cast off all shame...'

'No, no, no, Klinevitch, I was ashamed up there all the same, but here I should like to cast off shame, I should like it awfully.'

'I understand, Klinevitch,' boomed the engineer, 'that you want to rearrange life here on new and rational principles.'

'Oh, I don't care a hang about that! For that we'll wait for Kudeyarov who was brought here yesterday. When he wakes he'll tell you all about it. He is such a personality, such a titanic personality! Tomorrow they'll bring along another natural scientist, I believe, an officer for certain, and three or four days later a journalist, and, I believe, his editor with him. But deuce take them all, there will be a little group of us anyway, and things will arrange themselves. Though meanwhile I don't want us to be telling lies. That's all I care about, for that is one thing that matters. One cannot exist on the surface without lying, for life and lying are synonymous, but here we will amuse ourselves by not lying. Hang it all, the grave has some value after all! We'll all tell our stories aloud, and we won't be ashamed of anything. First of all I'll tell you about myself. I am one of the predatory kind, you know. All that was bound and held in check by rotten cords up there on the surface. Away with cords and let us spend these two months in shameless truthfulness! Let us strip and be naked!'

'Let us be naked, let us be naked!' cried all the voices.

'I long to be naked, I long to be,' Avdotya Ignatyevna shrilled.

'Ah...ah, I see we shall have fun here; I don't want Ecke after all.'

'No, I tell you. Give me a taste of life!'

'He-he-he!' giggled Katiche.

'The great thing is that no one can interfere with us, and though I see Pervoyedov is in a temper, he can't reach me with his hand. Grand-père, do you agree?'

'I fully agree, fully, and with the utmost satisfaction, but on condition that Katiche is the first to give us her biography.'

'I protest! I protest with all my heart!' General Pervoyedov brought out firmly.

'Your Excellency!' the scoundrel Lebeziatnikov persuaded him in a murmur of fussy excitement, 'your Excellency, it will be to our advantage to agree. Here, you see, there's this girl's... and all their little affairs.'

'There's the girl, it's true, but...'

'It's to our advantage, your Excellency, upon my word it is! If only as an experiment, let us try it...'

'Even in the grave they won't let us rest in peace.'

'In the first place, General, you were playing preference in the grave, and in the second we don't care a hang about you,' drawled Klinevitch.

'Sir, I beg you not to forget yourself.'

'What? Why, you can't get at me, and I can tease you from here as though you were Julie's lapdog. And another thing, gentlemen, how is he a general here? He was a general there, but here is mere refuse.'

'No, not mere refuse... Even here...'

'Here you will rot in the grave and six brass buttons will be all that will be left of you.'

'Bravo, Klinevitch, ha-ha-ha!' roared voices.

'I have served my sovereign... I have the sword...'

'Your sword is only fit to prick mice, and you never drew it even for that.'

'That makes no difference; I formed a part of the whole.'

'There are all sorts of parts in a whole.'

'Bravo, Klinevitch, bravo! Ha-ha-ha!'

'I don't understand what the sword stands for,' boomed the engineer.

'We shall run away from the Prussians like mice, they'll crush us to powder!' cried a voice in the distance that was unfamiliar to me, that was positively spluttering with glee.

'The sword, sir, is an honour,' the general cried, but only I heard him. There arose a prolonged and furious roar, clamour, and hubbub, and only the hysterically impatient squeals of Avdotya Ignatyevna were audible.

'But do let us make haste! Ah, when are we going to begin to cast off all shame!'

'Oh-ho-ho!... The soul does in truth pass through torments!' exclaimed the voice of the plebeian, 'and...'

And here I suddenly sneezed. It happened suddenly and unintentionally, but the effect was striking: all became as silent as one expects it to be in a churchyard, it all vanished like a dream. A real silence of the tomb set in. I don't believe they were ashamed on account of my presence: they had made up their minds to cast off all shame! I waited five minutes—not a word, not a sound. It cannot be supposed that they were afraid of my informing the police; for what could the police do to them? I must conclude that they had some secret unknown to the living, which they carefully concealed from every mortal.

'Well, my dears,' I thought, 'I shall visit you again.' And with those words, I left the cemetery.

No, that I cannot admit; no, I really cannot! The bobok case does not trouble me (so that is what that bobok signified!).

Depravity in such a place, depravity of the last aspirations, depravity of sodden and rotten corpses—and not even sparing the last moments of consciousness! Those moments have been granted, vouchsafed to them, and...and, worst of all, in such a place! No, that I cannot admit.

I shall go to other tombs, I shall listen everywhere. Certainly one ought to listen everywhere and not merely at one spot in order to form an idea. Perhaps one may come across something reassuring.

But I shall certainly go back to those. They promised their biographies and anecdotes of all sorts. Tfoo! But I shall go, I shall certainly go; it is a question of conscience!

I shall take it to the *Citizen*; the editor there has had his portrait exhibited too. Maybe he will print it.

6

THE DREAM OF A RIDICULOUS MAN

I

I am a ridiculous person. Now they call me a madman. That would be a promotion if it were not that I remain as ridiculous in their eyes as before. But now I do not resent it, they are all dear to me now, even when they laugh at me—and, indeed, it is just then that they are particularly dear to me. I could join in their laughter—not exactly at myself, but through affection for them, if I did not feel so sad as I look at them. Sad because they do not know the truth and I do know it. Oh, how hard it is to be the only one who knows the truth! But they won't understand that. No, they won't understand it.

In old days I used to be miserable at seeming ridiculous. Not seeming, but being. I have always been ridiculous, and I have known it, perhaps, from the hour I was born. Perhaps from the time I was seven years old I knew I was ridiculous. Afterwards I went to school, studied at the university, and, do you know, the more I learned, the more thoroughly I understood that I was ridiculous. So that it seemed in the end as though all the sciences I studied at the university existed only to prove and make evident to me as I went more deeply into them that I was ridiculous. It was the same with life as it was with science.

With every year the same consciousness of the ridiculous figure I cut in every relation grew and strengthened. Every one always laughed at me. But not one of them knew or guessed that if there were one man on earth who knew better than anybody else that I was absurd, it was myself, and what I resented most of all was that they did not know that. But that was my own fault; I was so proud that nothing would have ever induced me to tell it to any one. This pride grew in me with the years; and if it had happened that I allowed myself to confess to any one that I was ridiculous, I believe that I should have blown out my brains the same evening. Oh, how I suffered in my early youth from the fear that I might give way and confess it to my schoolfellows. But since I grew to manhood, I have for some unknown reason become calmer, though I realized my awful characteristic more fully every year. I say 'unknown,' for to this day I cannot tell why it was. Perhaps it was owing to the terrible misery that was growing in my soul through something which was of more consequence than anything else about me: that something was the conviction that had come upon me that *nothing in the world mattered*. I had long had an inkling of it, but the full realization came last year almost suddenly. I suddenly felt that it was all the same to me whether the world existed or whether there had never been anything at all: I began to feel with all my being that there was *nothing existing*. At first I fancied that many things had existed in the past, but afterwards I guessed that there never had been anything in the past either, but that it had only seemed so for some reason. Little by little I guessed that there would be nothing in the future either. Then I left off being angry with people and almost ceased to notice them. Indeed this showed itself even in the pettiest trifles: I used, for instance, to knock against people in the street. And not so much from being lost in thought: what had I to think about? I had almost given up thinking by that time; nothing mattered to me. If at least I had solved my problems! Oh, I had not settled one of them, and how many they were! But I gave up caring about anything, and all the problems disappeared.

And it was after that that I found out the truth. I learnt the truth last November—on the third of November, to be precise—and I remember every instant since. It was a gloomy evening, one of the gloomiest possible evenings. I was going home at about eleven o'clock, and I remember that I thought that the evening could not be gloomier. Even physically. Rain had been falling all day, and it had been a cold, gloomy, almost menacing rain, with, I remember, an unmistakable spite against mankind. Suddenly between ten and eleven it had stopped, and was followed by a horrible dampness, colder and damper than the rain, and a sort of steam was rising from everything, from every stone in the street, and from every by-lane if one looked down it as far as one could. A thought suddenly occurred to me, that if all the street lamps had been put out it would have been less cheerless, that the gas made one's heart sadder because it lighted it all up. I had had scarcely any dinner that day, and had been spending the evening with an engineer, and two other friends had been there also. I sat silent—I fancy I bored them. They talked of something rousing and suddenly they got excited over it. But they did not really care, I could see that, and only made a show of being excited. I suddenly said as much to them. 'My friends,' I said, 'you really do not care one way or the other.' They were not offended, but they all laughed at me. That was because I spoke without any note of reproach, simply because it did not matter to me. They saw it did not, and it amused them.

As I was thinking about the gas lamps in the street I looked up at the sky. The sky was horribly dark, but one could distinctly see tattered clouds, and between them fathomless black patches. Suddenly I noticed in one of these patches a star, and began watching it intently. That was because that star gave me an idea: I decided to kill myself that night. I had firmly determined to do so two months before, and poor as I was, I bought a splendid revolver that very day, and loaded it. But two months had passed and it was still lying in my drawer; I was so utterly indifferent that I wanted to seize a moment when I would not be so indifferent—why, I don't know. And so for two months every night that I came home I thought I would shoot myself. I kept waiting for the right moment. And so now this star gave me a thought. I made up my mind that it should certainly be that night. And why the star gave me the thought I don't know.

And just as I was looking at the sky, this little girl took me by the elbow. The street was empty, and there was scarcely any one to be seen. A cabman was sleeping in the distance in his cab. It was a child of eight with a kerchief on her head, wearing nothing but a wretched little dress all soaked with rain, but I noticed particularly her wet broken shoes and I recall them now. They caught my eye particularly. She suddenly pulled me by the elbow and called me. She was not weeping, but was spasmodically crying out some words which she could not utter properly, because she was shivering and shuddering all over. She was in terror about something, and kept crying, 'Mammy, mammy!' I turned facing her, I did not say a word and went on; but she ran, pulling at me, and there was that note in her voice which in frightened children means despair. I know that sound. Though she did not articulate the words, I understood that her mother was dying, or that something of the sort was happening to them, and that she had run out to call some one, to find something to help her mother. I did not go with her; on the contrary, I had an impulse to drive her away. I told her first to go to a policeman. But clasping her hands, she ran beside me sobbing and gasping, and would not leave me. Then I stamped my foot, and shouted at her. She called out 'Sir! sir!...' but suddenly abandoned me and rushed headlong across the road. Some other passer-by appeared there, and she evidently flew from me to him.

I mounted up to my fifth storey. I have a room in a flat where there are other lodgers. My room is small and poor, with a garret window in the shape of a semicircle. I have a sofa covered with American leather, a table with books on it, two chairs and a comfortable armchair, as old as old can be, but of the good old-fashioned shape. I sat down, lighted the candle, and began thinking. In the room next to mine, through the partition wall, a perfect Bedlam was going on. It had been going on for the last three days. A retired captain lived there, and he had half a dozen visitors, gentlemen of doubtful reputation, drinking vodka and playing stoss with old cards. The night before there had been a fight, and I know that two of them had been for a long time engaged in dragging each other about by the hair. The landlady wanted to complain, but she was in abject terror of the captain. There was only one other lodger in the flat, a thin little regimental lady, on a visit to Petersburg, with three little children who had been taken ill since they came into the lodgings. Both she and her children were in mortal fear of the captain, and lay trembling and crossing themselves all night, and the youngest child had a sort of fit from fright. That captain, I know for a fact, sometimes stops people in the Nevsky Prospect and begs. They won't take him into the service, but strange to say (that's why I am telling this), all this month that the captain has been here his behaviour has caused me no annoyance. I have, of course, tried to avoid his acquaintance from the very beginning, and he, too, was bored with me from the first; but I never care how much they shout the other side of the partition nor how many of them there are in there: I sit up all night and forget them so completely that I do not even hear them. I stay awake till daybreak, and have been going on like that for the last year. I sit up all night in my armchair at the table, doing nothing. I only read by day. I sit—don't even think; ideas of a sort wander through my mind and I let them come and go as they will. A whole candle is burnt every night. I sat down quietly at the table, took out the revolver and put it down before me. When I had put it down I asked myself, I remember, 'Is that so?' and answered with complete conviction, 'It is.' That is, I shall shoot myself. I knew that I should shoot myself that night for certain, but how much longer I should go on sitting at the table I did not know. And no doubt I should have shot myself if it had not been for that little girl.

II

You see, though nothing mattered to me, I could feel pain, for instance. If any one had struck me it would have hurt me. It was the same morally: if anything very pathetic happened, I should have felt pity just as I used to do in old days when there were things in life that did matter to me. I had felt pity that evening. I should have certainly helped a child. Why, then, had I not helped the little girl? Because of an idea that occurred to me at the time: when she was calling and pulling at me, a question suddenly arose before me and I could not settle it. The question was an idle one, but I was vexed. I was vexed at the reflection that if I were going to make an end of myself that night, nothing in life ought to have mattered to me. Why was it that all at once I did not feel that nothing mattered and was sorry for the little girl? I remember that I was very sorry for her, so much so that I felt a strange pang, quite incongruous in my position. Really I do not know better how to convey my fleeting sensation at the moment, but the sensation persisted at home when I was sitting at the table, and I was very much irritated as I had not been for a long time past. One reflection followed another. I saw clearly that so long as I was still a human being and not nothingness, I was alive and so could suffer, be angry and feel shame at my actions. So be it. But if I am going to kill myself, in two hours, say, what is the little girl to me and what have I to do with shame or with anything else in the world? I shall turn into nothing, absolutely nothing. And can it really be true that the consciousness that I shall *completely* cease to exist immediately and so everything else will cease to exist, does not in the least affect my feeling of pity for the child nor the feeling of shame after a contemptible action? I stamped and shouted at the unhappy child as though to say—not only I feel no pity, but even if I behave inhumanly and contemptibly, I am free to, for in another two hours everything will be extinguished. Do you believe that that was why I shouted that? I am almost convinced of it now. It seemed clear to me that life and the world somehow depended upon me now. I may almost say that the world now seemed created for me alone: if I shot myself the world would cease to be at least for me. I say nothing of its being likely that nothing will exist for any one when I am gone, and that as soon as my consciousness is extinguished the whole world will vanish too and become void like a phantom, as a mere appurtenance of my consciousness, for possibly all this world and all these people are only me myself. I remember that as I sat and reflected, I turned all these new questions that swarmed one after another quite the other way, and thought of something quite new. For instance, a strange reflection suddenly occurred to me, that if I had lived before on the moon or on Mars and there had committed the most disgraceful and dishonourable action and had there been put to such shame and ignominy as one can only conceive and realize in dreams, in nightmares, and if, finding myself afterwards on earth, I were able to retain the memory of what I had done on the other planet and at the same time knew that I should never, under any circumstances, return there, then looking from the earth to the moon—*should I care or not?* Should I feel shame for that action or not? These were idle and superfluous questions for the revolver was already lying before me, and I knew in every fibre of my being that it would happen for certain, but they excited me and I raged. I could not die now without having first settled something. In short, the child had saved me, for I put off my pistol shot for the sake of these questions. Meanwhile the clamour had begun to subside in the captain's room: they had finished their game, were settling down to sleep, and meanwhile were grumbling and languidly winding up their quarrels. At that point I suddenly fell asleep in my chair at the table—a thing which had never happened to me before. I dropped asleep quite unawares.

Dreams, as we all know, are very queer things: some parts are presented with appalling vividness, with details worked up with the elaborate finish of jewellery, while others one gallops through, as it were, without noticing them at all, as, for instance, through space and time. Dreams seem to be spurred on not by reason but by desire, not by the head but by the heart, and yet what complicated tricks my reason has played sometimes in dreams, what utterly incomprehensible things happen to it! My brother died five years ago, for instance. I sometimes dream of him; he takes part in my affairs, we are very much interested, and yet all through my dream I quite know and remember that my brother is dead and buried. How is it that I am not surprised that, though he is dead, he is here beside me and working with me? Why is it that my reason fully accepts it? But enough. I will begin about my dream. Yes, I dreamed a dream, my dream of the third of November. They tease me now, telling me it was only a dream. But does it matter whether it was a dream or reality, if the dream made known to me the truth? If once one has recognized the truth and seen it, you know that it is the truth and that there is no other and there cannot be, whether you are asleep or awake. Let it be a dream, so be it, but that real life of which you make so much I had meant to extinguish by suicide, and my dream, my dream—oh, it revealed to me a different life, renewed, grand and full of power!

Listen.

III

I have mentioned that I dropped asleep unawares and even seemed to be still reflecting on the same subjects. I suddenly dreamt that I picked up the revolver and aimed it straight at my heart—my heart, and not my head; and I had determined beforehand to fire at my head, at my right temple. After aiming at my chest I waited a second or two, and suddenly my candle, my table, and the wall in front of me began moving and heaving. I made haste to pull the trigger.

In dreams you sometimes fall from a height, or are stabbed, or beaten, but you never feel pain unless, perhaps, you really bruise yourself against the bedstead, then you feel pain and almost always wake up from it. It was the same in my dream. I did not feel any pain, but it seemed as though with my shot everything within me was shaken and everything was suddenly dimmed, and it grew horribly black around me. I seemed to be blinded and benumbed, and I was lying on something hard, stretched on my back; I saw nothing, and could not make the slightest movement. People were walking and shouting around me, the captain bawled, the landlady shrieked—and suddenly another break and I was being carried in a closed coffin. And I felt how the coffin was shaking and reflected upon it, and for the first time the idea struck me that I was dead, utterly dead, I knew it and had no doubt of it, I could neither see nor move and yet I was feeling and reflecting. But I was soon reconciled to the position, and as one usually does in a dream, accepted the facts without disputing them.

And now I was buried in the earth. They all went away, I was left alone, utterly alone. I did not move. Whenever before I had imagined being buried the one sensation I associated with the grave was that of damp and cold. So now I felt that I was very cold, especially the tips of my toes, but I felt nothing else.

I lay still, strange to say I expected nothing, accepting without dispute that a dead man had nothing to expect. But it was damp. I don't know how long a time passed—whether an hour, or several days, or many days. But all at once a drop of water fell on my closed left eye, making its way through a coffin lid; it was followed a minute later by a second, then a minute later by a third—and so on, regularly every minute. There was a sudden glow of profound indignation in my heart, and I suddenly felt in it a pang of physical pain. 'That's my wound,' I thought; 'that's the bullet...' And drop after drop every minute kept falling on my closed eyelid. And all at once, not with my voice, but with my whole being, I called upon the power that was responsible for all that was happening to me:

'Whoever you may be, if you exist, and if anything more rational than what is happening here is possible, suffer it to be here now. But if you are revenging yourself upon me for my senseless suicide by the hideousness and absurdity of this subsequent existence, then let me tell you that no torture could ever equal the contempt which I shall go on dumbly feeling, though my martyrdom may last a million years!'

I made this appeal and held my peace. There was a full minute of unbroken silence and again another drop fell, but I knew with infinite unshakable certainty that everything would change immediately. And behold my grave suddenly was rent asunder, that is, I don't know whether it was opened or dug up, but I was caught up by some dark and unknown being and we found ourselves in space. I suddenly regained my sight. It was the dead of night, and never, never had there been such darkness. We were flying through space far away from the earth. I did not question the being who was taking me; I was proud and waited. I assured myself that I was not afraid, and was thrilled with ecstasy at the thought that I was not afraid. I do not know how long we were flying, I cannot imagine; it happened as it always does in dreams when you skip over space and time, and the laws of thought and existence, and only pause upon the points for which the heart yearns. I remember that I suddenly saw in the darkness a star. 'Is that Sirius?' I asked impulsively, though I had not meant to ask any questions.

'No, that is the star you saw between the clouds when you were coming home,' the being who was carrying me replied.

I knew that it had something like a human face. Strange to say, I did not like that being, in fact I felt an intense aversion for it. I had expected complete non-existence, and that was why I had put a bullet through my heart. And here I was in the hands of a creature not human, of course, but yet living, existing. 'And so there is life beyond the grave,' I thought with the strange frivolity one has in dreams. But in its inmost depth my heart remained unchanged. 'And if I have got to exist again,' I thought, 'and live once more under the control of some irresistible power, I won't be vanquished and humiliated.'

'You know that I am afraid of you and despise me for that,' I said suddenly to my companion, unable to refrain from the humiliating question which implied a confession, and feeling my humiliation stab my heart as with a pin. He did not answer my question, but all at once I felt that he was not even despising me, but was laughing at me and had no compassion for me, and that our journey had an unknown and mysterious object that concerned me only. Fear was growing in my heart. Something was mutely and painfully communicated to me from my silent companion, and permeated my whole being. We were flying through dark, unknown space. I had for some time lost sight of the constellations familiar to my eyes. I knew that there were stars in the heavenly spaces the light of which took thousands or millions of years to reach the earth. Perhaps we were already flying through those spaces. I expected something with a terrible anguish that tortured my heart. And suddenly I was thrilled by a familiar feeling that stirred me to the depths: I suddenly caught sight of our sun! I knew that it could not be *our* sun, that gave life to *our* earth, and that we were an infinite distance from our sun, but for some reason I knew in my whole being that it was a sun exactly like ours, a duplicate of it. A sweet, thrilling feeling resounded with ecstasy in my heart: the kindred power of the same light which had given me light stirred an echo in my heart and awakened it, and I had a sensation of life, the old life of the past for the first time since I had been in the grave.

'But if that is the sun, if that is exactly the same as our sun,' I cried, 'where is the earth?'

And my companion pointed to a star twinkling in the distance with an emerald light. We were flying straight towards it.

'And are such repetitions possible in the universe? Can that be the law of Nature?... And if that is an earth there, can it be just the same earth as ours...just the same, as poor, as unhappy, but precious and beloved for ever, arousing in the most ungrateful of her children the same poignant love for her that we feel for our earth?' I cried out, shaken by irresistible, ecstatic love for the old familiar earth which I had left. The image of the poor child whom I had repulsed flashed through my mind.

'You shall see it all,' answered my companion, and there was a note of sorrow in his voice.

But we were rapidly approaching the planet. It was growing before my eyes; I could already distinguish the ocean, the outline of Europe; and suddenly a feeling of a great and holy jealousy glowed in my heart.

'How can it be repeated and what for? I love and can love only that earth which I have left, stained with my blood, when, in my ingratitude, I quenched my life with a bullet in my heart. But I have never, never ceased to love that earth, and perhaps on the very night I parted from it I loved it more than ever. Is there suffering upon this new earth? On our earth we can only love with suffering and through suffering. We cannot love otherwise, and we know of no other sort of love. I want suffering in order to love. I long, I thirst, this very instant, to kiss with tears the earth that I have left, and I don't want, I won't accept life on any other!'

But my companion had already left me. I suddenly, quite without noticing how, found myself on this other earth, in the bright light of a sunny day, fair as paradise. I believe I was standing on one of the islands that make up on our globe the Greek archipelago, or on the coast of the mainland facing that archipelago. Oh, everything was exactly as it is with us, only everything seemed to have a festive radiance, the splendour of some great, holy triumph attained at last. The caressing sea, green as emerald, splashed softly upon the shore and kissed it with manifest, almost conscious love. The tall, lovely trees stood in all the glory of their blossom, and their innumerable leaves greeted me, I am certain, with their soft, caressing rustle and seemed to articulate words of love. The grass glowed with bright and fragrant flowers. Birds were flying in flocks in the air, and perched fearlessly on my shoulders and arms and joyfully struck me with their darling, fluttering wings. And at last I saw and knew the people of this happy land. They came to me of themselves, they surrounded me, kissed me. The children of the sun, the children of their sun—oh, how beautiful they were! Never had I seen on our own earth such beauty in mankind. Only perhaps in our children, in their earliest years, one might find some remote, faint reflection of this beauty. The eyes of these happy people shone with a clear brightness. Their faces were radiant with the light of reason and fullness of a serenity that comes of perfect understanding, but those faces were gay; in their words and voices there was a note of childlike joy. Oh, from the first moment, from the first glance at them, I understood it all! It was the earth untarnished by the Fall; on it lived people who had not sinned. They lived just in such a paradise as that in which, according to all the legends of mankind, our first parents lived before they sinned; the only difference was that all this earth was the same paradise. These people, laughing joyfully, thronged round me and caressed me; they took me home with them, and each of them tried to reassure me. Oh, they asked me no questions, but they seemed, I fancied, to know everything without asking, and they wanted to make haste and smoothe away the signs of suffering from my face.

IV

And do you know what? Well, granted that it was only a dream, yet the sensation of the love of those innocent and beautiful people has remained with me for ever, and I feel as though their love is still flowing out to me from over there. I have seen them myself, have known them and been convinced; I loved them, I suffered for them afterwards. Oh, I understood at once even at the time that in many things I could not understand them at all; as an up-to-date Russian progressive and contemptible Petersburger, it struck me as inexplicable that, knowing so much, they had, for instance, no science like ours. But I soon realized that their knowledge was gained and fostered by intuitions different from those of us on earth, and that their aspirations, too, were quite different. They desired nothing and were at peace; they did not aspire to knowledge of life as we aspire to understand it, because their lives were full. But their knowledge was higher and deeper than ours; for our science seeks to explain what life is, aspires to understand it in order to teach others how to live, while they without science knew how to live; and that I understood, but I could not understand their knowledge. They showed me their trees, and I could not understand the intense love with which they looked at them; it was as though they were talking with creatures like themselves. And perhaps I shall not be mistaken if I say that they conversed with them. Yes, they had found their language, and I am convinced that the trees understood them. They looked at all Nature like that—at the animals who lived in peace with them and did not attack them, but loved them, conquered by their love. They pointed to the stars and told me something about them which I could not understand, but I am convinced that they were somehow in touch with the stars, not only in thought, but by some living channel. Oh, these people did not persist in trying to make me understand them, they loved me without that, but I knew that they would never understand me, and so I hardly spoke to them about our earth. I only kissed in their presence the earth on which they lived and mutely worshipped them themselves. And they saw that and let me worship them without being abashed at my adoration, for they themselves loved much. They were not unhappy on my account when at times I kissed their feet with tears, joyfully conscious of the love with which they would respond to mine. At times I asked myself with wonder how it was they were able never to offend a creature like me, and never once to arouse a feeling of jealousy or envy in me? Often I wondered how it could be that, boastful and untruthful as I was, I never talked to them of what I knew—of which, of course, they had no notion—that I was never tempted to do so by a desire to astonish or even to benefit them.

They were as gay and sportive as children. They wandered about their lovely woods and copses, they sang their lovely songs; their fare was light—the fruits of their trees, the honey from their woods, and the milk of the animals who loved them. The work they did for food and raiment was brief and not laborious. They loved and begot children, but I never noticed in them the impulse of that *cruel* sensuality which overcomes almost every man on this earth, all and each, and is the source of almost every sin of mankind on earth. They rejoiced at the arrival of children as new beings to share their happiness. There was no quarrelling, no jealousy among them, and they did not even know what the words meant. Their children were the children of all, for they all made up one family. There was scarcely any illness among them, though there was death; but their old people died peacefully, as though falling asleep, giving blessings and smiles to those who surrounded them to take their last farewell with bright and loving smiles. I never saw grief or tears on those occasions, but only love, which reached the point of ecstasy, but a calm ecstasy, made perfect and contemplative. One might think that they were still in contact with the departed after death, and that their earthly union was not cut short by death. They scarcely understood me when I questioned them about immortality, but evidently they were so convinced of it without reasoning that it was not for them a question at all. They had no temples, but they had a real living and uninterrupted sense of oneness with the whole of the universe; they had no creed, but they had a certain knowledge that when their earthly joy had reached the limits of earthly nature, then there would come for them, for the living and for the dead, a still greater fullness of contact with the whole of the universe. They looked forward to that moment with joy, but without haste, not pining for it, but seeming to have a foretaste of it in their hearts, of which they talked to one another.

In the evening before going to sleep they liked singing in musical and harmonious chorus. In those songs they expressed all the sensations that the parting day had given them, sang its glories and took leave of it. They sang the praises of nature, of the sea, of the woods. They liked making songs about one another, and praised each other like children; they were the simplest songs, but they sprang from their hearts and went to one's heart. And not only in their songs but in all their lives they seemed to do nothing but admire one another. It was like being in love with each other, but an all-embracing, universal feeling.

Some of their songs, solemn and rapturous, I scarcely understood at all. Though I understood the words I could never fathom their full significance. It remained, as it were, beyond the grasp of my mind, yet my heart unconsciously absorbed it more and more. I often told them that I had had a presentiment of it long before, that this joy and glory had come to me on our earth in the form of a yearning melancholy that at times approached insufferable sorrow; that I had had a foreknowledge of them all and of their glory in the dreams of my heart and the visions of my mind; that often on our earth I could not look at the setting sun without tears...that in my hatred for the men of our earth there was always a yearning anguish: why could I not hate them without loving them? why could I not help forgiving them? and in my love for them there was a yearning grief: why could I not love them without hating them? They listened to me, and I saw they could not conceive what I was saying, but I did not regret that I had spoken to them of it: I knew that they understood the intensity of my yearning anguish over those whom I had left. But when they looked at me with their sweet eyes full of love, when I felt that in their presence my heart, too, became as innocent and just as theirs, the feeling of the fullness of life took my breath away, and I worshipped them in silence.

Oh, every one laughs in my face now, and assures me that one cannot dream of such details as I am telling now, that I only dreamed or felt one sensation that arose in my heart in delirium and made up the details myself when I woke up. And when I told them that perhaps it really was so, my God, how they shouted with laughter in my face, and what mirth I caused! Oh, yes, of course I was overcome by the mere sensation of my dream, and that was all that was preserved in my cruelly wounded heart; but the actual forms and images of my dream, that is, the very ones I really saw at the very time of my dream, were filled with such harmony, were so lovely and enchanting and were so actual, that on awakening I was, of course, incapable of clothing them in our poor language, so that they were bound to become blurred in my mind; and so perhaps I really was forced afterwards to make up the details, and so of course to distort them in my passionate desire to convey some at least of them as quickly as I could. But on the other hand, how can I help believing that it was all true? It was perhaps a thousand times brighter, happier and more joyful than I describe it. Granted that I dreamed it, yet it must have been real. You know, I will tell you a secret: perhaps it was not a dream at all! For then something happened so awful, something so horribly true, that it could not have been imagined in a dream. My heart may have originated the dream, but would my heart alone have been capable of originating the awful event which happened to me afterwards? How could I alone have invented it or imagined it in my dream? Could my petty heart and my fickle, trivial mind have risen to such a revelation of truth? Oh, judge for yourselves: hitherto I have concealed it, but now I will tell the truth. The fact is that I…corrupted them all!

V

Yes, yes, it ended in my corrupting them all! How it could come to pass I do not know, but I remember it clearly. The dream embraced thousands of years and left in me only a sense of the whole. I only know that I was the cause of their sin and downfall. Like a vile trichina, like a germ of the plague infecting whole kingdoms, so I contaminated all this earth, so happy and sinless before my coming. They learnt to lie, grew fond of lying, and discovered the charm of falsehood. Oh, at first perhaps it began innocently, with a jest, coquetry, with amorous play, perhaps indeed with a germ, but that germ of falsity made its way into their hearts and pleased them. Then sensuality was soon begotten, sensuality begot jealousy, jealousy—cruelty... Oh, I don't know, I don't remember; but soon, very soon the first blood was shed. They marvelled and were horrified, and began to be split up and divided. They formed into unions, but it was against one another. Reproaches, upbraidings followed. They came to know shame, and shame brought them to virtue. The conception of honour sprang up, and every union began waving its flags. They began torturing animals, and the animals withdrew from them into the forests and became hostile to them. They began to struggle for separation, for isolation, for individuality, for mine and thine. They began to talk in different languages. They became acquainted with sorrow and loved sorrow; they thirsted for suffering, and said that truth could only be attained through suffering. Then science appeared. As they became wicked they began talking of brotherhood and humanitarianism, and understood those ideas. As they became criminal, they invented justice and drew up whole legal codes in order to observe it, and to ensure their being kept, set up a guillotine. They hardly remembered what they had lost, in fact refused to believe that they had ever been happy and innocent.

They even laughed at the possibility of this happiness in the past, and called it a dream. They could not even imagine it in definite form and shape, but, strange and wonderful to relate, though they lost all faith in their past happiness and called it a legend, they so longed to be happy and innocent once more that they succumbed to this desire like children, made an idol of it, set up temples and worshipped their own idea, their own desire; though at the same time they fully believed that it was unattainable and could not be realized, yet they bowed down to it and adored it with tears! Nevertheless, if it could have happened that they had returned to the innocent and happy condition which they had lost, and if some one had shown it to them again and had asked them whether they wanted to go back to it, they would certainly have refused. They answered me:

'We may be deceitful, wicked and unjust, we *know* it and weep over it, we grieve over it; we torment and punish ourselves more perhaps than that merciful Judge Who will judge us and whose Name we know not. But we have science, and by means of it we shall find the truth and we shall arrive at it consciously. Knowledge is higher than feeling, the consciousness of life is higher than life. Science will give us wisdom, wisdom will reveal the laws, and the knowledge of the laws of happiness is higher than happiness.'

That is what they said, and after saying such things every one began to love himself better than any one else, and indeed they could not do otherwise. All became so jealous of the rights of their own personality that they did their very utmost to curtail and destroy them in others, and made that the chief thing in their lives. Slavery followed, even voluntary slavery; the weak eagerly submitted to the strong, on condition that the latter aided them to subdue the still weaker. Then there were saints who came to these people, weeping, and talked to them of their pride, of their loss of harmony and due proportion, of their loss of shame. They were laughed at or pelted with stones. Holy blood was shed on the threshold of the temples. Then there arose men who began to think how to bring all people together again, so that everybody, while still loving himself best of all, might not interfere with others, and all might live together in something like a harmonious society. Regular wars sprang up over this idea. All the combatants at the same time firmly believed that science, wisdom and the instinct of self-preservation would force men at last to unite into a harmonious and rational society; and so, meanwhile, to hasten matters, 'the wise' endeavoured to exterminate as rapidly as possible all who were 'not wise' and did not understand their idea, that the latter might not hinder its triumph. But the instinct of self-preservation grew rapidly weaker; there arose men, haughty and sensual, who demanded all or nothing. In order to obtain everything they resorted to crime, and if they did not succeed—to suicide. There arose religions with a cult of non-existence and self-destruction for the sake of the everlasting peace of annihilation. At last these people grew weary of their meaningless toil, and signs of suffering came into their faces, and then they proclaimed that suffering was a beauty, for in suffering alone was there meaning. They glorified suffering in their songs. I moved about among them, wringing my hands and weeping over them, but I loved them perhaps more than in old days when there was no suffering in their faces and when they were innocent and so lovely. I loved the earth they had polluted even more than when it had been a paradise, if only because sorrow had come to it. Alas! I always loved sorrow and tribulation, but only for myself, for myself; but I wept over them, pitying them. I stretched out my hands to them in despair, blaming, cursing and despising myself. I told them that all this was my doing, mine alone; that it was I had brought them corruption, contamination and falsity. I besought them to crucify me, I taught them how to make a cross. I could not kill myself, I had not the strength, but I wanted to suffer at their hands. I yearned for suffering, I longed that my blood should be drained to the last drop in these agonies. But they only laughed at me, and began at last to look upon me as crazy. They justified me, they declared that they had only got what they wanted themselves, and that all that now was could not have been otherwise. At last they declared to me that I was becoming dangerous and that they should lock me up in a madhouse if I did not hold my tongue. Then such grief took possession of my soul that my heart was wrung, and I felt as though I were dying; and then...then I awoke.

It was morning, that is, it was not yet daylight, but about six o'clock. I woke up in the same armchair; my candle had burnt out; every one was asleep in the captain's room, and there was a stillness all round, rare in our flat. First of all I leapt up in great amazement: nothing like this had ever happened to me before, not even in the most trivial detail; I had never, for instance, fallen asleep like this in my armchair. While I was standing and coming to myself I suddenly caught sight of my revolver lying loaded, ready—but instantly I thrust it away! Oh, now, life, life! I lifted up my hands and called upon eternal truth, not with words but with tears; ecstasy, immeasurable ecstasy flooded my soul. Yes, life and spreading the good tidings! Oh, I at that moment resolved to spread the tidings, and resolved it, of course, for my whole life. I go to spread the tidings, I want to spread the tidings—of what? Of the truth, for I have seen it, have seen it with my own eyes, have seen it in all its glory.

And since then I have been preaching! Moreover I love all those who laugh at me more than any of the rest. Why that is so I do not know and cannot explain, but so be it. I am told that I am vague and confused, and if I am vague and confused now, what shall I be later on? It is true indeed: I am vague and confused, and perhaps as time goes on I shall be more so. And of course I shall make many blunders before I find out how to preach, that is, find out what words to say, what things to do, for it is a very difficult task. I see all that as clear as daylight, but, listen, who does not make mistakes? And yet, you know, all are making for the same goal, all are striving in the same direction anyway, from the sage to the lowest robber, only by different roads. It is an old truth, but this is what is new: I cannot go far wrong. For I have seen the truth; I have seen and I know that people can be beautiful and happy without losing the power of living on earth. I will not and cannot believe that evil is the normal condition of mankind. And it is just this faith of mine that they laugh at. But how can I help believing it? I have seen the truth—it is not as though I had invented it with my mind, I have seen it, seen it, and the living image of it has filled my soul for ever. I have seen it in such full perfection that I cannot believe that it is impossible for people to have it. And so how can I go wrong? I shall make some slips no doubt, and shall perhaps talk in second-hand language, but not for long: the living image of what I saw will always be with me and will always correct and guide me. Oh, I am full of courage and freshness, and I will go on and on if it were for a thousand years! Do you know, at first I meant to conceal the fact that I corrupted them, but that was a mistake—that was my first mistake! But truth whispered to me that I was lying, and preserved me and corrected me. But how establish paradise—I don't know, because I do not know how to put it into words. After my dream I lost command of words. All the chief words, anyway, the most necessary ones. But never mind, I shall go and I shall keep talking, I won't leave off, for anyway I have seen it with my own eyes, though I cannot describe what I saw. But the scoffers do not understand that. It was a dream, they say, delirium, hallucination. Oh! As though that meant so much! And they are so proud! A dream! What is a dream? And is not our life a dream? I will say more. Suppose that this paradise will never come to pass (that I understand), yet I shall go on preaching it. And yet how simple it is: in one day, *in one hour* everything could be arranged at once! The chief thing is to love others like yourself, that's the great thing, and that's everything; nothing else is wanted—you will find out at once how to arrange it all. And yet it's an old truth which has been told and retold a billion times—but it has not formed part of our lives! The consciousness of life is higher than life, the knowledge of the laws of happiness is higher than happiness—that is what one must contend against. And I shall. If only every one wants it, it can all be arranged at once.

And I tracked out that little girl...and I shall go on and on!